12

IRISH
GHOST
STORIES

Patricia Craig was born and educated in Belfast before
moving to London where she now lives. She is a freelance
critic and reviewer and has edited several anthologies
including Oxford Books of *English Detective Stories*, *Travel
Stories*, and *Modern Women's Stories*.

Oxford Twelves

Twelve Mystery Stories
JACK ADRIAN

Twelve Tales of Murder
JACK ADRIAN

Twelve Tales of the Supernatural
MICHAEL COX

Twelve Victorian Ghost Stories
MICHAEL COX

Twelve Irish Ghost Stories
PATRICIA CRAIG

Twelve American Crime Stories
ROSEMARY HERBERT

Twelve American Detective Stories
EDWARD D. HOCH

Twelve Women Detective Stories
LAURA MARCUS

Forthcoming:

Twelve English Detective Stories
MICHAEL COX

Twelve Gothic Tales
RICHARD DALBY

12

IRISH
GHOST STORIES

Selected and introduced by

PATRICIA CRAIG

Oxford   New York

OXFORD UNIVERSITY PRESS

1998

Oxford University Press, Great Clarendon Street, Oxford OX2 6DP

Oxford New York

Athens Auckland Bangkok Bogota Bombay
Buenos Aires Calcutta Cape Town Dar es Salaam
Delhi Florence Hong Kong Istanbul Karachi
Kuala Lumpur Madras Madrid Melbourne
Mexico City Nairobi Paris Singapore
Taipei Tokyo Toronto Warsaw

and associated companies in
Berlin Ibadan

Oxford is a trade mark of Oxford University Press

First published as an Oxford University Press paperback 1998

British Library Cataloguing in Publication Data
Data available

Library of Congress Cataloging in Publication Data
Twelve Irish ghost stories / selected and introduced by Patricia Craig.
(Oxford twelves)
1. Ghosts stories, English—Irish authors. 2. English fiction—Irish authors.
I. Craig, Patricia. II. Series.
PR8876.5.G45T87 1998   823'.0877308941⁵—dc21   97-34563
ISBN 0-19-288070-5 (pbk)

1 3 5 7 9 10 8 6 4 2

Typeset by Jayvee, Trivandrum, India
Printed in Great Britain by
Cox & Wyman, Reading
England

CONTENTS

Introduction   vii

1

CECIL FRANCES ALEXANDER (1818–95)
The Legend of Stumpie's Brae (c.1839)
1

2

J. SHERIDAN LE FANU (1814–73)
*An Account of Some Strange Disturbances
in Aungier Street (1853)*
7

3

CHARLOTTE RIDDELL (1832–1906)
The Last of Squire Ennismore (1888)
29

4

ROSA MULHOLLAND (1841–1921)
The Ghost at the Rath (1891)
37

5

GEORGE MOORE (1852–1933)
A Play-House in the Waste (1903)
57

6

FORREST REID (1875–1947)
Courage (1918)
68

Contents

7

DOROTHY MACARDLE (1889–1958)
The Prisoner (1924)
76

8

ELIZABETH BOWEN (1899–1973)
The Happy Autumn Fields (1945)
83

9

J. F. BYRNE (1880–1955)
'Ghosts' in House on Cork Hill (1953)
101

10

SHANE LESLIE (1885–1971)
A Laugh on the Professor (1955)
109

11

PETER SOMERVILLE-LARGE (1928–   )
Rich and Strange (1977)
115

12

MAURICE LEITCH (1933–   )
Green Roads (1987)
129

Biographical Notes   143

Source Acknowledgements   145

INTRODUCTION

Heard ye no' tell of the Stumpie's Brae?
  Sit down, sit down, young friend,
I'll make your flesh to creep to-day,
  And your hair to stan' on end.

This declaration of intent by Cecil Frances Alexander (1818–95) neatly sums up the aim of every ghost-story writer: to induce in readers extremes of delectable dread. The old dark house, the uncanny infestation, the step on the stair: these figments have exercised the imagin-ations of avid readers from the early nine-teenth century on. But hair-raising is only the start of it. The super-natural story can, and does, accommodate a whole range of tones, from the grisly comic (as with Mrs Alexander, above) to the sociologically and psychologically chilling (as in George Moore's 'A Play-House in the Waste'). This short collection of Irish stories underscores another point: that all kinds of larger preoccupations, on the part of the author, may find an outlet in this enticing brand of genre fiction. Irish ghosts, to a notable extent, are tied up with Irish history; indeed, you might say there's a sense in which the whole country is haunted by its past.

You might go further and speculate whether this general haunt-ing, along with a feeling for the numinous which extends to pre-Christian and fairy lore, hasn't somehow militated in Ireland against the develop-ment of a formidable body of supernatural fic-tion. It has to be said that the Irish, so celebrated for their mastery of the short story as a literary form, aren't by and large great ghost-story writers. Aside from Sheridan Le Fanu, there is no one whose name is definitively, and exclusively, associated with the genre—as, say, that of M. R. James or H. Russell Wakefield in England. There are obvious reasons for this. As English society became more secu-lar and rational, from about the 1890s on, the supernatural, in compensation, gained an increasing fascination as a literary topic; whereas in Ireland—where every ruined abbey, deserted house, lichened graveyard, or crumbling wall has a story attached to it—it was either taken so much for granted as to seem unworthy of special emphasis, or repudiated, on the other hand, as the residue of a primitive past. Either way, it didn't suggest itself strongly as a fictional theme.

Readers of this anthology, however, will be left in no doubt that exceptions *did* occur, or that certain Irish stories can take their place among the triumphs of the ghost genre. 'The Happy Autumn Fields', by Elizabeth Bowen (to take that example), is a marvel of subtlety and pungent dislocation, with its—unspecified—Co. Cork setting superimposed over a ravaged London, *c*.1940. The George Moore contribution ('A Play-House in the Waste') is dense with implications: a puritan society, roads going nowhere, the continual defeat of every liberal impulse. Its pathetic apparition ('a white thing gliding') somehow gets to the heart of backwardness and desolation. A lesser story, 'The Ghost at the Rath' by Rosa Mulholland, is none the less to be savoured for its deployment of every full-blown supernatural effect. A sinister inheritance, an isolated mansion, leads to vivid dreams for the protagonist (dreams which curiously recall the experiences of humans lured into fairy mounds), while the ghostly re-enactment of a crime achieves a striking reversal of injustice, in the best manner of the Victorian 'sensation' mode. The Le Fanu story, 'An Account of Some Strange Disturbances in Aungier Street', has all the classic ingredients—the old town house, alarms in the night, a malevolent apparition, a diabolical rat—and an investigative alertness to boot. Another Dublin house, this time on Cork Hill, is the scene of the one non-fictional episode (by J. F. Byrne) in this collection—included because it has all the shimmer and coherence of a piece of imaginative writing. This particular blighted house turns out to have connections with the Phoenix Park murderers of 1882—Carey and the rest of them—a circumstance which adds historical resonance, the one quality which is almost *de rigueur* in Irish ghost-story writing.

So, we find Dorothy Macardle, the official historian of the War of Independence, focusing (in 'The Prisoner') on the glamour of the unimpeachable cause, and also on the ineradicable opprobrium, in Irish minds, attaching to the word 'informer'. A place of bygone slaughter on the Kerry coast is at the centre of Peter Somerville-Large's 'Rich and Strange', in which a young girl on holiday comes up smack against the lacerating past. And Maurice Leitch's 'Green Roads'—which brings us up to the present, with the British Army in the North—gets all kinds of reverberations into its account of a suicide, a dimly recollected tale concerning Pikemen and Fencibles, people caught up in some kind of on-going historical imperative. This story is very adroit and mysterious.

What else? Shane Leslie provides advice for guests at Irish castles who shouldn't make assumptions about the provenance of uncommunicative footmen. Mrs Alexander, taking time off from her hymn-writing, narrates in verse a fearsome retribution tale involving a mutilated pedlar. These, in their different ways, are *jeux d'esprit* and carry no charnel charge whatever. Squire Ennismore, in the story by Mrs Riddell, is another matter: here, there's some hellish business afoot. And Forrest Reid's 'Courage': this, with its heightened calm and lucidity, generates a distinctly spooky feeling ('The greyness ended at the first landing; beyond that, an impenetrable blackness led to those awful upper storeys') for most of its length, sufficient to nullify the odd touch of sentimentality which creeps in along with the supernatural *frisson*. All these stories, I would contend, have their own integrity as exercises in the eerie, take a spirited approach to the spirits they evoke, and remain endlessly intriguing.

I should like to thank Richard Dalby for some sound advice and practical help. And I am, as ever, grateful to Jeffrey Morgan for encouragement and moral support.

PATRICIA CRAIG
London, 1997

THE TRAMP AND THE GHOST

A tramp was promised 'a lump of money' if he would agree to stay in a haunted house. He agrees. He has been provided with a good fire, with food, drink, and tobacco, and is left alone. He bars the door.

Around midnight he takes off one of his boots. He is taking off the other when he hears a sound behind him. He looks . . . and sees a tall, dark man hovering above him.

'You're alone,' says the stranger.

'Yes,' says the tramp, 'and as soon as I get this boot back on you'll be alone too.'

MICHAEL J. MURPHY, *Now You're Talking; Folk Tales from the North of Ireland* (Blackstaff 1975)

1

CECIL FRANCES ALEXANDER

The Legend of Stumpie's Brae*

Heard ye no' tell of the Stumpie's Brae?
    Sit down, sit down, young friend,
I'll make your flesh to creep today,
    And your hair to stan' on end.

Young man, it's hard to strive wi' sin,
    And the hardest strife of a'
Is where the greed o' gain creeps in,
    And drives God's grace awa'.

Oh, it's quick to do, but it's lang to rue,
    When the punishment comes at last,
And we would give the world to undo
    The deed that's done and past.

Over yon strip of meadow land,
    And over the burnie bright,
Dinna ye mark the fir-trees stand,
    Around yon gable white?

I mind it weel, in my younger days
    The story yet was rife:

* This ballad embodies an actual legend attached to a lonely spot on the border of
the county of Donegal. The *language* of the ballad is the peculiar semi-Scottish dialect
spoken in the north of Ireland.

There dwelt within that lonely place
    A farmer man and his wife.

They sat together all alone,
    One blessed autumn night,
When the trees without, and hedge, and stone,
    Were white in the sweet moonlight.

The boys and girls were gone down all
    A wee to the blacksmith's wake;
There pass'd ane on by the window small,
    And guv the door a shake.

The man he up and open'd the door—
    When he had spoken a bit,
A pedlar men stepp'd into the floor,
Down he tumbled the pack he bore,
    Right heavy pack was it.

'Gude save us a',' says the wife, wi' a smile,
    'But yours is a thrivin' trade.'—
'Ay, ay, I've wander'd mony a mile,
    And plenty have I made.'

The man sat on by the dull fire flame,
    When the pedlar went to rest;
Close to his ear the Devil came,
    And slipp'd intil his breast.

He look'd at his wife by the dim fire light,
    And she was as bad as he—
'Could we no' murder thon man the night?'—
    'Ay, could we, ready,' quo' she.

He took the pickaxe without a word,
    Whence it stood, ahint the door;

2

As he pass'd in, the sleeper stirr'd,
   That never waken'd more.

'He's dead!' says the auld man, coming back—
   'What o' the corp, my dear?'
'We'll bury him snug in his ain bit pack,
Never ye mind for the loss of the sack,
   I've ta'en out a' the gear.'

'The pack's owre short by twa gude span,
   What'll we do?' quo' he—
'Oh, you're a doited, unthoughtfu' man,
   We'll cut him off at the knee.'

They shorten'd the corp, and they pack'd him tight,
   Wi' his legs in a pickle hay;
Over the burn, in the sweet moonlight,
   They carried him till this brae.

They shovell'd a hole right speedily,
   They laid him in on his back—
'A right pair are ye,' quo' the PEDLAR, quo' he,
   Sitting bolt upright in the pack.

'Ye think ye've laid me snugly here,
   And none shall know my station;
But I'll hant ye far, and I'll hant ye near,
Father and son, wi' terror and fear,
   To the nineteenth generation.'

The twa were sittin' the vera next night,
   When the dog began to cower,
And they knew, by the pale blue fire light,
   That the Evil One had power.

It had stricken nine, just nine o' the clock—

The hour when the man lay dead;
There came to the outer door a knock,
  And a heavy, heavy tread.

The old man's head swam round and round,
  The woman's blood 'gan freeze,
For it was not like a natural sound,
But like some one stumping o'er the ground
  An the banes of his twa bare knees.

And through the door, like a sough of air,
  And stump, stump, round the twa,
Wi' his bloody head, and his knee banes bare—
  They'd maist ha'e died of awe!

The wife's black locks ere morn grew white,
  They say, as the mountain snaws;
The man was as straight as a staff that night,
  But he stoop'd when the morning rose.

Still, year and day, as the clock struck NINE,
  The hour when they did the sin,
The wee bit dog began to whine,
  And the ghaist came clattering in.

Ae night there was a fearful flood—
  Three days the skies had pour'd;
And white wi' foam, and black wi' mud,
  The burn in fury roar'd.

Quo' she—'Gude man, ye need na turn
  Sae pale in the dim fire light;
The Stumpie canna cross the burn,
  He'll no' be here the night.

'For it's o'er the bank, and it's o'er the linn,
  And it's up to the meadow ridge—'

'Ay,' quo' the Stumpie hirpling in,
And he gied the wife a slap on the chin,
   'But *I cam' round by the bridge!*'*

And stump, stump, stump, to his plays again,
   And o'er the stools and chairs;
Ye'd surely hae thought ten women and men
   Were dancing there in pairs.

They sold their gear, and over the sea
   To a foreign land they went,
Over the sea—but wha can flee
   His appointed punishment?

The ship swam over the water clear,
   Wi' the help o' the eastern breeze;
But the vera first sound in guilty fear,
O'er the wide, smooth deck, that fell on their ear
   Was the tapping o' them twa knees.

In the woods of wild America
   Their weary feet they set;
But Stumpie was there the first, they say,
And he haunted them on to their dying day,
   And he follows their children yet.

I haud ye, never the voice of blood
   Call'd from the earth in vain;
And never has crime won worldly good,
   But it brought its after-pain.

This is the story o' Stumpie's Brae,
   And the murderers' fearfu' fate:
Young man, your face is turn'd that way,
   Ye'll be ganging the night that gate.

       * So in the legend.

Ye'll ken it weel, through the few fir trees,
   The house where they wont to dwell;
Gin ye meet ane there, as daylight flees,
Stumping about on the banes of his knees,
   It'll jist be Stumpie himsel'.

J. SHERIDAN LE FANU

An Account of Some Strange Disturbances in Aungier Street

It is not worth telling, this story of mine—at least, not worth writing. Told, indeed, as I have sometimes been called upon to tell it, to a circle of intelligent and eager faces, lighted up by a good after-dinner fire on a winter's evening, with a cold wind rising and wailing outside, and all snug and cosy within, it has gone off—though I say it, who should not—indifferent well. But it is a venture to do as you would have me. Pen, ink, and paper are cold vehicles for the marvellous, and a 'reader' decidedly a more critical animal than a 'listener'. If, however, you can induce your friends to read it after nightfall, and when the fireside talk has run for a while on thrilling tales of shapeless terror; in short, if you will secure me the *mollia tempora fandi*, I will go to my work, and say my say, with better heart. Well, then, these conditions presupposed, I shall waste no more words, but tell you simply how it all happened.

My cousin (Tom Ludlow) and I studied medicine together. I think he would have succeeded, had he stuck to the profession; but he preferred the Church, poor fellow, and died early, a sacrifice to contagion, contracted in the noble discharge of his duties. For my present purpose, I say enough of his character when I mention that he was of a sedate but frank and cheerful nature; very exact in his observance of truth, and not by any means like myself—of an excitable or nervous temperament.

My Uncle Ludlow—Tom's father—while we were attending

lectures, purchased three or four old houses in Aungier Street, one of which was unoccupied. *He* resided in the country, and Tom proposed that we should take up our abode in the untenanted house, so long as it should continue unlet; a move which would accomplish the double end of settling us nearer alike to our lecture-rooms and to our amusements, and of relieving us from the weekly charge of rent for our lodgings.

Our furniture was very scant—our whole equipage remarkably modest and primitive; and, in short, our arrangements pretty nearly as simple as those of a bivouac. Our new plan was, therefore, executed almost as soon as conceived. The front drawing-room was our sitting-room. I had the bedroom over it, and Tom the back bedroom on the same floor, which nothing could have induced me to occupy.

The house, to begin with, was a very old one. It had been, I believe, newly fronted about fifty years before; but with this exception, it had nothing modern about it. The agent who bought it and looked into the titles for my uncle, told me that it was sold, along with much other forfeited property, at Chichester House, I think, in 1702, and had belonged to Sir Thomas Hacket, who was Lord Mayor of Dublin in James II's time. How old it was *then*, I can't say; but, at all events, it had seen years and changes enough to have contracted all that mysterious and saddened air, at once exciting and depressing, which belongs to most old mansions.

There had been very little done in the way of modernizing details; and, perhaps, it was better so; for there was something queer and bygone in the very walls and ceilings—in the shape of doors and windows—in the odd diagonal site of the chimney-pieces—in the beams and ponderous cornices—not to mention the singular solidity of all the woodwork, from the banisters to the window-frames, which hopelessly defied disguise, and would have emphatically proclaimed their antiquity through any conceivable amount of modern finery and varnish.

An effort had, indeed, been made, to the extent of papering the drawing-rooms; but somehow, the paper looked raw and out of keeping; and the old woman, who kept a little dirt-pie of a shop in the lane, and whose daughter—a girl of two and fifty—was our solitary handmaid, coming in at sunrise, and chastely receding again as soon as she had made all ready for tea in our state apartment;—this woman, I say, remembered it, when old Judge Horrocks (who, having earned the reputation of a particularly 'hanging judge', ended by hanging himself, as the coroner's jury found, under an impulse of 'temporary insanity', with a child's skipping-rope, over the massive old banisters) resided there, entertaining good company, with fine venison and rare old port. In those halcyon days, the drawing-rooms were hung with gilded leather, and, I dare say, cut a good figure, for they were really spacious rooms.

The bedrooms were wainscoted, but the front one was not gloomy; and in it the cosiness of antiquity quite overcame its sombre associations. But the back bedroom, with its two queerly placed melancholy windows, staring vacantly at the foot of the bed, and with the shadowy recess to be found in most old houses in Dublin, like a large ghostly closet, which, from congeniality of temperament, had amalgamated with the bedchamber, and dissolved the partition. At night-time, this 'alcove'—as our 'maid' was wont to call it—had, in my eyes, a specially sinister and suggestive character. Tom's distant and solitary candle glimmered vainly into its darkness. *There* it was always overlooking him—always itself impenetrable. But this was only part of the effect. The whole room was, I can't tell how, repulsive to me. There was, I suppose, in its proportions and features, a latent discord—a certain mysterious and indescribable relation, which jarred indistinctly upon some secret sense of the fitting and the safe, and raised indefinable suspicions and apprehensions of the imagination. On the whole, as I began by saying, nothing could have induced me to pass a night alone in it.

I had never pretended to conceal from poor Tom my superstitious weakness; and he, on the other hand, most unaffectedly ridiculed my tremors. The sceptic was, however, destined to receive a lesson, as you shall hear.

We had not been very long in occupation of our respective dormitories, when I began to complain of uneasy nights and disturbed sleep. I was, I suppose, the more impatient under this annoyance, as I was usually a sound sleeper, and by no means prone to nightmares. It was now, however, my destiny, instead of enjoying my customary repose, every night to 'sup full of horrors'. After a preliminary course of disagreeable and frightful dreams, my troubles took a definite form, and the same vision, without an appreciable variation in a single detail, visited me at least (on an average) every second night in the week.

Now, this dream, nightmare, or infernal illusion—which you please—of which I was the miserable sport, was on this wise—

I saw, or thought I saw, with the most abominable distinctness, although at the time in profound darkness, every article of furniture and accidental arrangement of the chamber in which I lay. This, as you know, is incidental to ordinary nightmare. Well, while in this clairvoyant condition, which seemed but the lighting up of the theatre in which was to be exhibited the monotonous tableau of horror, which made my nights insupportable, my attention invariably became, I know not why, fixed upon the windows opposite the foot of my bed; and, uniformly with the same effect, a sense of dreadful anticipation always took slow but sure possession of me. I became somehow conscious of a sort of horrid but undefined preparation going forward in some unknown quarter, and by some unknown agency, for my torment; and, after an interval, which always seemed to me of the same length, a picture suddenly flew up to the window, where it remained fixed, as if by an electrical attraction, and my discipline of horror then commenced, to last perhaps for hours. The picture thus mysteriously glued to the window-panes, was the portrait of an old man, in a crimson flowered silk dressing-gown, the folds of which I could now describe, with a countenance embodying a strange mixture of intellect, sensuality, and power, but withal sinister and full of malignant omen. His nose was hooked, like the beak of a vulture; his eyes large, grey, and prominent, and lighted up with a more than mortal cruelty and coldness. These features were surmounted by a crimson velvet cap, the hair that peeped from under which was white with age, while the eyebrows retained their original blackness. Well I remember every line, hue, and shadow of that stony countenance, and well I may! The gaze of this hellish visage was fixed upon me, and mine returned it with the inexplicable fascination of nightmare, for what appeared to me to be hours of agony. At last—

'The cock he crew, away then flew'

the fiend who had enslaved me through the awful watches of the night; and, harassed and nervous, I rose to the duties of the day.

I had—I can't say exactly why, but it may have been from the exquisite anguish and profound impressions of unearthly horror, with which this strange phantasmagoria was associated—an insurmountable antipathy to describing the exact nature of my nightly troubles to my friend and comrade. Generally, however, I told him that I was haunted by abominable dreams; and, true to the imputed materialism of medicine, we put our heads together to dispel my horrors, not by exorcism, but by a tonic.

I will do this tonic justice, and frankly admit that the accursed portrait began to intermit its visits under its influence. What of that? Was this singular apparition—as full of character as of terror—therefore the creature of my fancy, or the invention of my poor stomach? Was it, in short, *subjective* (to borrow the technical slang of the day) and not the palpable aggression and intrusion of an external agent? That, good friend, as we will both admit, by no means follows. The evil spirit, who enthralled my senses in the shape of that portrait, may have been just as near me, just as energetic, just as malignant, though I saw him not. What means the whole moral code of revealed religion regarding the due keeping of our own bodies, soberness, temperance, etc.? Here is an obvious connection between the material and the invisible; the healthy tone of the system, and its unimpaired energy, may, for aught we can tell, guard us against influences which would otherwise render life itself terrific. The mesmerist and the electro-biologist will fail upon an average with nine patients out of ten—so may the evil spirit. Special conditions of the corporeal system are indispensable to the production of certain spiritual phenomena. The operation succeeds sometimes—sometimes fails—that is all.

I found afterwards that my would-be sceptical companion had

his troubles too. But of these I knew nothing yet. One night, for a wonder, I was sleeping soundly, when I was roused by a step on the lobby outside my room, followed by the loud clang of what turned out to be a large brass candlestick, flung with all his force by poor Tom Ludlow over the banisters, and rattling with a rebound down the second flight of stairs; and almost concurrently with this, Tom burst open my door, and bounced into my room backwards, in a state of extraordinary agitation.

I had jumped out of bed and clutched him by the arm before I had any distinct idea of my own whereabouts. There we were—in our shirts—standing before the open door—staring through the great old banister opposite, at the lobby window, through which the sickly light of a clouded moon was gleaming.

'What's the matter, Tom? What's the matter with you? What the devil's the matter with you, Tom?' I demanded shaking him with nervous impatience.

He took a long breath before he answered me, and then it was not very coherently.

'It's nothing, nothing at all—did I speak?—what did I say?—where's the candle, Richard? It's dark; I—I had a candle!'

'Yes, dark enough,' I said; 'but what's the matter?—what *is* it?—why don't you speak, Tom?—have you lost your wits?—what is the matter?'

'The matter?—oh, it is all over. It must have been a dream—nothing at all but a dream—don't you think so? It could not be anything more than a dream.'

'Of *course*,' said I, feeling uncommonly nervous, 'it *was* a dream.'

'I thought,' he said, 'there was a man in my room, and—and I jumped out of bed; and—and—where's the candle?'

'In your room, most likely,' I said, 'shall I go and bring it?'

'No; stay here—don't go; it's no matter—don't, I tell you; it was all a dream. Bolt the door, Dick; I'll stay here with you—I feel nervous. So, Dick, like a good fellow, light your candle and open the window—I am in a *shocking state*.'

I did as he asked me, and robing himself like Granuaile in one of my blankets, he seated himself close beside my bed.

Everybody knows how contagious is fear of all sorts, but more especially that particular kind of fear under which poor Tom was at that moment labouring. I would not have heard, nor I believe would he have recapitulated, just at that moment, for half the world, the details of the hideous vision which had so unmanned him.

'Don't mind telling me anything about your nonsensical dream, Tom,' said I, affecting contempt, really in a panic; 'let us talk about something else; but it is quite plain that this dirty old house disagrees with us both, and hang me if I stay here any longer, to be pestered with indigestion and—and—bad nights, so we may as well look out for lodgings—don't you think so?—at once.'

Tom agreed, and, after an interval, said—

'I have been thinking, Richard, that it is a long time since I saw my father, and I have made up my mind to go down tomorrow and return in a day or two, and you can take rooms for us in the meantime.'

I fancied that this resolution, obviously the result of the vision which had so profoundly scared him, would probably vanish next morning with the damps and shadows of night. But I was mistaken. Off went Tom at peep of day to the country, having agreed that so soon as I had secured suitable lodgings, I was to recall him by letter from his visit to my Uncle Ludlow.

Now, anxious as I was to change my quarters, it so happened, owing to a series of petty procrastinations and accidents, that nearly a week elapsed before my bargain was made and my letter of recall on the wing to Tom; and, in the meantime, a trifling adventure or two had occurred to your humble servant, which, absurd as they now appear, diminished by distance, did certainly at the time serve to whet my appetite for change considerably.

A night or two after the departure of my comrade, I was sitting by my bedroom fire, the door locked, and the ingredients of a tumbler of hot whisky-punch upon the crazy spider-table; for, as the best mode of keeping the

'Black spirits and white,
Blue spirits and grey,'

13

with which I was environed, at bay, I had adopted the practice recommended by the wisdom of my ancestors, and 'kept my spirits
up by pouring spirits down'. I had thrown aside my volume of
Anatomy, and was treating myself by way of a tonic, preparatory
to my punch and bed, to half-a-dozen pages of the *Spectator*, when
I heard a step on the flight of stairs descending from the attics. It
was two o'clock, and the streets were as silent as a churchyard—
the sounds were, therefore, perfectly distinct. There was a slow,
heavy tread, characterized by the emphasis and deliberation of
age, descending by the narrow staircase from above; and, what
made the sound more singular, it was plain that the feet which produced it were perfectly bare, measuring the descent with something between a pound and a flop, very ugly to hear.

I knew quite well that my attendant had gone away many hours
before, and that nobody but myself had any business in the house.
It was quite plain also that the person who was coming downstairs
had no intention whatever of concealing his movements; but, on
the contrary, appeared disposed to make even more noise, and pro-
ceed more deliberately, than was at all necessary. When the step
reached the foot of the stairs outside my room, it seemed to stop;
and I expected every moment to see my door open spontaneously,
and give admission to the original of my detested portrait. I was,
however, relieved in a few seconds by hearing the descent
renewed, just in the same manner, upon the staircase leading
down to the drawing-rooms, and thence, after another pause,
down the next flight, and so on to the hall, whence I heard no
more.

Now, by the time the sound had ceased, I was wound up, as they
say, to a very unpleasant pitch of excitement. I listened, but there
was not a stir. I screwed up my courage to a decisive experiment—
opened my door, and in a stentorian voice bawled over the banisters, 'Who's there?' There was no answer but the ringing of my
own voice through the empty old house—no renewal of the movement; nothing, in short, to give my unpleasant sensations a
definite direction. There is, I think, something most disagreeably
disenchanting in the sound of one's own voice under such circum-

stances, exerted in solitude, and in vain. It redoubled my sense of isolation, and my misgivings increased on perceiving that the door, which I certainly thought I had left open, was closed behind me; in a vague alarm, lest my retreat should be cut off, I got again into my room as quickly as I could, where I remained in a state of imaginary blockade, and very uncomfortable indeed, till morning.

Next night brought no return of my barefooted fellow-lodger; but the night following, being in my bed, and in the dark—somewhere, I suppose, about the same hour as before, I distinctly heard the old fellow again descending from the garrets.

This time I had had my punch, and the *morale* of the garrison was consequently excellent. I jumped out of bed, clutched the poker as I passed the expiring fire, and in a moment was upon the lobby. The sound had ceased by this time—the dark and chill were discouraging; and, guess my horror, when I saw, or thought I saw, a black monster, whether in the shape of a man or a bear I could not say, standing, with its back to the wall, on the lobby, facing me, with a pair of great greenish eyes shining dimly out. Now, I must be frank, and confess that the cupboard which displayed our plates and cups stood just there, though at the moment I did not recollect it. At the same time I must honestly say, that making every allowance for an excited imagination, I never could satisfy myself that I was made the dupe of my own fancy in this matter; for this apparition, after one or two shiftings of shape, as if in the act of incipient transformation, began, as it seemed on second thoughts, to advance upon me in its original form. From an instinct of terror rather than of courage, I hurled the poker, with all my force, at its head; and to the music of a horrid crash made my way into my room, and double-locked the door. Then, in a minute more, I heard the horrid bare feet walk down the stairs, till the sound ceased in the hall, as on the former occasion.

If the apparition of the night before was an ocular delusion of my fancy sporting with the dark outlines of our cupboard, and if its horrid eyes were nothing but a pair of inverted teacups, I had, at all events, the satisaction of having launched the poker with admirable effect, and in true 'fancy' phrase, 'knocked its two daylights into one', as the commingled fragments of my tea-service testified. I did my best to gather comfort and courage from these evidences; but it would not do. And then what could I say of those horrid bare feet, and the regular tramp, tramp, tramp, which measured the distance of the entire staircase through the solitude of my haunted dwelling, and at an hour when no good influence was stirring? Confound it!—the whole affair was abominable. I was out of spirits, and dreaded the approach of night.

It came, ushered ominously in with a thunderstorm and dull torrents of depressing rain. Earlier than usual the streets grew silent; and by twelve o'clock nothing but the comfortless pattering of the rain was to be heard.

I made myself as snug as I could. I lighted *two* candles instead of one. I forswore bed, and held myself in readiness for a sally, candle in hand; for, *coute qui coute*, I was resolved to *see* the being, if visible at all, who troubled the nightly stillness of my mansion. I was fidgetty and nervous and, tried in vain to interest myself with my books. I walked up and down my room, whistling in turn martial and hilarious music, and listening ever and anon for the dreaded noise. I sat down and stared at the square label on the solemn and reserved-looking black bottle, until 'FLANAGAN & CO.'S BEST OLD MALT WHISKY' grew into a sort of subdued accompaniment to all the fantastic and horrible speculations which chased one another through my brain.

Silence, meanwhile, grew more silent, and darkness darker. I listened in vain for the rumble of a vehicle, or the dull clamour of a distant row. There was nothing but the sound of a rising wind, which had succeeded the thunderstorm that had travelled over the Dublin mountains quite out of hearing. In the middle of this great city I began to feel myself alone with nature, and Heaven knows what beside. My courage was ebbing. Punch, however, which makes beasts of so many, made a man of me again—just in time to hear with tolerable nerve and firmness the lumpy, flabby, naked feet deliberately descending the stairs again.

I took a candle, not without a tremor. As I crossed the floor I tried to extemporize a prayer, but stopped short to listen, and never finished it. The steps continued. I confess I hesitated for some seconds at the door before I took heart of grace and opened it. When I peeped out the lobby was perfectly empty—there was no monster standing on the staircase; and as the detested sound ceased, I was reassured enough to venture forward nearly to the banisters. Horror of horrors! within a stair or two beneath the spot where I stood the unearthly tread smote the floor. My eye caught something in motion; it was about the size of Goliath's foot—it was grey, heavy, and flapped with a dead weight from one step to another. As I am alive, it was the most monstrous grey rat I ever beheld or imagined.

Shakespeare says—'Some men there are cannot abide a gaping pig, and some that are mad if they behold a cat.' I went well-nigh out of my wits when I beheld this *rat*; for, laugh at me as you may, it fixed upon me, I thought, a perfectly human expression of malice; and, as it shuffled about and looked up into my face almost from between my feet, I saw, I could swear it—I felt it then, and know it now, the infernal gaze and the accursed countenance of my old friend in the portrait, transfused into the visage of the bloated vermin before me.

I bounced into my room again with a feeling of loathing and horror I cannot describe, and locked and bolted my door as if a lion had been at the other side. D——n him or *it*; curse the portrait and its original! I felt in my soul that the rat—yes, the *rat*, the RAT I had just seen, was that evil being in masquerade, and rambling through the house upon some infernal night lark.

Next morning I was early trudging through the miry streets; and, among other transactions, posted a peremptory note recalling Tom. On my return, however, I found a note from my absent 'chum', announcing his intended return next day. I was doubly rejoiced at this, because I had succeeded in getting rooms; and because the change of scene and return of my comrade were rendered specially pleasant by the last night's half ridiculous half horrible adventure.

I slept extemporaneously in my new quarters in Digges' Street that night, and next morning returned for breakfast to the haunted mansion, where I was certain Tom would call immediately on his arrival.

I was quite right—he came; and almost his first question referred to the primary object of our change of residence.

'Thank God,' he said with genuine fervour, on hearing that all was arranged. 'On *your* account I am delighted. As to myself, I assure you that no earthly consideration could have induced me ever again to pass a night in this disastrous old house.'

'Confound the house!' I ejaculated, with a genuine mixture of fear and detestation, 'we have not had a pleasant hour since we came to live here'; and so I went on, and related incidentally my adventure with the plethoric old rat.

'Well, if that were *all*,' said my cousin, affecting to make light of the matter, 'I don't think I should have minded it very much.'

'Ay, but its eye—its countenance, my dear Tom,' urged I; 'if you had seen *that*, you would have felt it might be *anything* but what it seemed.'

'I inclined to think the best conjurer in such a case would be an able-bodied cat,' he said, with a provoking chuckle.

'But let us hear your own adventure,' I said tartly.

At this challenge he looked uneasily round him. I had poked up a very unpleasant recollection.

'You shall hear it, Dick; I'll tell it to you,' he said. 'Begad, sir, I should feel quite queer, though, telling it *here*, though we are too strong a body for ghosts to meddle with just now.'

Though he spoke this like a joke, I think it was serious calculation. Our Hebe was in a corner of the room, packing our cracked delft tea- and dinner-services in a basket. She soon suspended operations, and with mouth and eyes wide open became an absorbed listener. Tom's experiences were told nearly in these words:

'I saw it three times, Dick—three distinct times; and I am perfectly certain it meant me some infernal harm. I was, I say, in danger—in *extreme* danger; for, if nothing else had happened, my reason would most certainly have failed me, unless I had escaped so soon. Thank God. I *did* escape.

'The first night of this hateful disturbance, I was lying in the attitude of sleep, in that lumbering old bed. I hate to think of it. I was really wide awake, though I had put out my candle, and was lying as quietly as if I had been asleep; and although accidentally restless, my thoughts were running in a cheerful and agreeable channel.

'I think it must have been two o'clock at least when I thought I heard a sound in that—that odious dark recess at the far end of the bedroom. It was as if someone was drawing a piece of cord slowly along the floor, lifting it up, and dropping it softly down again in coils. I sat up once or twice in my bed, but could see nothing, so I concluded it must be mice in the wainscot. I felt no emotion graver than curiosity, and after a few minutes ceased to observe it.

'While lying in this state, strange to say, without at first a suspicion of anything supernatural, on a sudden I saw an old man, rather stout and square, in a sort of roan-red dressing-gown, and with a black cap on his head, moving stiffly and slowly in a diagonal direction, from the recess, across the floor of the bedroom, passing my bed at the foot, and entering the lumber-closet at the left. He had something under his arm; his head hung a little at one side; and, merciful God! When I saw his face.'

Tom stopped for a while, and then said—

'That awful countenance, which living or dying I never can forget, disclosed what he was. Without turning to the right or left, he passed beside me, and entered the closet by the bed's head.

'While this fearful and indescribable type of death and guilt was passing, I felt that I had no more power to speak or stir than if I had been myself a corpse. For hours after it had disappeared, I was too terrified and weak to move. As soon as daylight came, I took courage, and examined the room, and especially the course which the frightful intruder had seemed to take, but there was not a vestige to indicate anybody's having passed there; no sign of any disturbing agency visible among the lumber that strewed the floor of the closet.

'I now began to recover a little. I was fagged and exhausted, and at last, overpowered by a feverish sleep. I came down late; and finding you out of spirits, on account of your dreams about the portrait, whose *original* I am now certain disclosed himself to me, I did not care to talk about the infernal vision. In fact, I was trying to persuade myself that the whole thing was an illusion, and I did not like to revive in their intensity the hated impressions of the past night—or, to risk the constancy of my scepticism, by recounting the tale of my sufferings.

'It required some nerve, I can tell you, to go to my haunted chamber next night, and lie down quietly in the same bed,' continued Tom. 'I did so with a degree of trepidation, which, I am not ashamed to say, a very little matter would have sufficed to stimulate to downright panic. This night, however, passed off quietly enough, as also the next; and so too did two or three more. I grew more confident, and began to fancy that I believed in the theories of spectral illusions, with which I had at first vainly tried to impose upon my convictions.

'The apparition had been, indeed, altogether anomalous. It had crossed the room without any recognition of my presence: I had not disturbed *it*, and *it* had no mission to *me*. What, then, was the imaginable use of its crossing the room in a visible shape at all? Of course it might have *been* in the closet instead of *going* there, as easily as it introduced itself into the recess without entering the chamber in a shape discernible by the senses. Besides, how the deuce *had* I seen it? It was a dark night; I had no candle; there was no fire; and yet I saw it as distinctly, in colouring and outline, as ever I beheld human form! A cataleptic dream would explain it all; and I was determined that a dream it should be.

'One of the most remarkable phenomena connected with the practice of mendacity is the vast number of deliberate lies we tell ourselves, whom, of all persons, we can least expect to deceive. In all this, I need hardly tell you, Dick, I was simply lying to myself, and did not believe one word of the wretched humbug. Yet I went on, as men will do, like persevering charlatans and impostors, who tire people into credulity by the mere force of reiteration; so I hoped to win myself over at last to a comfortable scepticism about the ghost.

'He had not appeared a second time—that certainly was a comfort; and what, after all, did I care for him, and his queer old toggery and strange looks? Not a fig! I was nothing the worse for having seen him, and a good story the better. So I tumbled into bed, put out my candle, and, cheered by a loud drunken quarrel in the back lane, went fast asleep.

'From this deep slumber I awoke with a start. I knew I had had a horrible dream; but what it was I could not remember. My heart was thumping furiously; I felt bewildered and feverish; I sat up in the bed and looked about the room. A broad flood of moonlight came in through the curtainless window; everything was as I had last seen it; and though the domestic squabble in the back lane was, unhappily for me, allayed, I yet could hear a pleasant fellow singing, on his way home, the then popular comic ditty called, "Murphy Delany". Taking advantage of this diversion I lay down again, with my face towards the fireplace, and closing my eyes, did my best to think of nothing else but the song, which was every moment growing fainter in the distance:

'Twas Murphy Delany, so funny and frisky,
   Stept into a shebeen shop to get his skin full;
He reeled out again pretty well lined with whiskey,
   As fresh as a shamrock, as blind as a bull.

'The singer, whose condition I dare say resembled that of his hero, was soon too far off to regale my ears any more; and as his music died away, I myself sank into a doze, neither sound nor refreshing. Somehow the song had got into my head, and I went meandering on through the adventures of my respectable fellow-countryman, who, on emerging from the "shebeen shop", fell into a river, from which he was fished up to be "sat upon" by a coroner's jury, who having learned from a "horse-doctor" that he was "dead as a door-nail, so there was an end", returned their verdict accordingly, just as he returned to his senses, when an angry altercation and a pitched battle between the body and the coroner winds up the lay with due spirit and pleasantry.

'Through this ballad I continued with a weary monotony to plod, down to the very last line, and then *da capo*, and so on, in my uncomfortable half-sleep, for how long, I can't conjecture. I found myself at last, however, muttering, "*dead* as a door-nail, so there was an end"; and something like another voice within me, seemed to say, very faintly, but sharply, "dead! dead! *dead!* and may the Lord have mercy on your soul!" and instantaneously I was wide awake, and staring right before me from the pillow.

'Now—will you believe it, Dick?—I saw the same accursed figure standing full front, and gazing at me with its stony and fiendish countenance, not two yards from the bedside.'

Tom stopped here, and wiped the perspiration from his face. I felt very queer. The girl was as pale as Tom; and, assembled as we were in the very scene of these adventures, we were all, I dare say, equally grateful for the clear daylight and the resuming bustle out of doors.

'For about three seconds only I saw it plainly; then it grew indistinct; but, for a long time, there was something like a column of dark vapour where it had been standing, between me and the wall; and I felt sure that he was still there. After a good while, this appearance went too. I took my clothes downstairs to the hall, and dressed there, with the door half open; then went out into the street, and walked about the town till morning, when I came back, in a miserable state of nervousness and exhaustion. I was such a fool, Dick, as to be ashamed to tell you how I came to be so upset. I thought you would laugh at me; especially as I had always talked philosophy, and treated *your* ghosts with contempt. I concluded you would give me no quarter; and so kept my tale of horror to myself.

'Now, Dick, you will hardly believe me, when I assure you, that for many nights after this last experience, I did not go to my room at all. I used to sit up for a while in the drawing-room after you had gone up to your bed; and then steal down softly to the hall-door, let myself out, and sit in the "Robin Hood" tavern until the last guest went off; and then I got through the night like a sentry, pacing the streets till morning.

'For more than a week I never slept in bed. I sometimes had a snooze on a form in the "Robin Hood", and sometimes a nap in a chair during the day; but regular sleep I had absolutely none.

'I was quite resolved that we should get into another house; but I could not bring myself to tell you the reason, and I somehow put it off from day to day, although my life was, during every hour of this procrastination, rendered as miserable as that of a felon with the constables on his track. I was growing absolutely ill from this wretched mode of life.

'One afternoon I determined to enjoy an hour's sleep upon your bed. I hated mine; so that I had never, except in a stealthy visit every day to unmake it, lest Martha should discover the secret of my nightly absence, entered the ill-omened chamber.

'As ill-luck would have it, you had locked your bedroom, and taken away the key. I went into my own to unsettle the bedclothes, as usual, and give the bed the appearance of having been slept in. Now, a variety of circumstances concurred to bring about the dreadful scene through which I was that night to pass. In the first place, I was literally overpowered with fatigue, and longing for sleep; in the next place, the effect of this extreme exhaustion upon my nerves resembled that of a narcotic, and rendered me less susceptible than, perhaps I should in any other condition have been, of the exciting fears which had become habitual to me. Then again, a little bit of the window was open, a pleasant freshness pervaded the room, and, to crown all, the cheerful sun of day was making the room quite pleasant. What was to prevent my enjoying an hour's nap *here?* The whole air was resonant with the cheerful hum of life, and the broad matter-of-fact light of day filled every corner of the room.

'I yielded—stifling my qualms—to the almost overpowering temptation; and merely throwing off my coat, and loosening my cravat, I lay down, limiting myself to *half*-an-hour's doze in the unwonted enjoyment of a feather bed, a coverlet, and a bolster.

'It was horribly insidious; and the demon, no doubt, marked my infatuated preparations. Dolt that I was, I fancied, with mind and body worn out for want of sleep, and an arrear of a full week's rest to my credit, that such measure as *half*-an-hour's sleep, in such a situation, was possible. My sleep was death-like, long, and dreamless.

'Without a start or fearful sensation of any kind, I waked

gently, but completely. It was, as you have good reason to remember, long past midnight—I believe, about two o'clock. When sleep has been deep and long enough to satisfy nature thoroughly, one often wakens in this way, suddenly, tranquilly, and completely.

'There was a figure seated in that lumbering, old sofa-chair, near the fireplace. Its back was rather towards me, but I could not be mistaken; it turned slowly round, and, merciful heavens! there was the stony face, with its infernal lineaments of malignity and despair, gloating on me. There was now no doubt as to its consciousness of my presence, and the hellish malice with which it was animated, for it arose, and drew close to the bedside. There was a rope about its neck, and the other end, coiled up, it held stiffly in its hand.

'My good angel nerved me for this horrible crisis. I remained for some seconds transfixed by the gaze of this tremendous phantom. He came close to the bed, and appeared on the point of mounting upon it. The next instant I was upon the floor at the far side, and in a moment more was, I don't know how, upon the lobby.

'But the spell was not yet broken; the valley of the shadow of death was not yet traversed. The abhorred phantom was before me there; it was standing near the banisters, stooping a little, and with one end of the rope round its own neck, was poising a noose at the other, as if to throw over mine; and while engaged in this baleful pantomime, it wore a smile so sensual, so unspeakably dreadful, that my senses were nearly overpowered. I saw and remember nothing more, until I found myself in your room.

'I had a wonderful escape, Dick—there is no disputing *that*—an escape for which, while I live, I shall bless the mercy of heaven. No one can conceive or imagine what it is for flesh and blood to stand in the presence of such a thing, but one who has had the terrific experience. Dick, Dick, a shadow has passed over me—a chill has crossed my blood and marrow, and I will never be the same again—never, Dick—never!'

Our handmaid, a mature girl of two-and-fifty, as I have said, stayed her hand, as Tom's story proceeded, and by little and little drew near to us, with open mouth, and her brows contracted over her little, beady black eyes, till stealing a glance over her shoulder now and then, she established herself close behind us. During the relation, she had made various earnest comments, in an undertone; but these and her ejaculations, for the sake of brevity and simplicity, I have omitted in my narration.

'It's often I heard tell of it,' she now said, 'but I never believed it rightly till now—though, indeed, why should not I? Does not my mother, down there in the lane, know quare stories, God bless us, beyant telling about it? But you ought not to have slept in the back bedroom. She was loath to let me be going in and out of that room even in the daytime, let alone for any Christian to spend the night in it; for sure she says it was his own bedroom.'

'*Whose* own bedroom?' we asked, in a breath.

'Why, *his*—the ould Judge's—Judge Horrock's, to be sure, God rest his sowl'; and she looked fearfully round.

'Amen!' I muttered. 'But did he die there?'

'Die there! No, not quite *there*,' she said. 'Shure, was not it over the banisters he hung himself, the ould sinner, God be merciful to us all? and was not it in the alcove they found the handles of the skipping-rope cut off, and the knife where he was settling the cord, God bless us, to hang himself with? It was his housekeeper's daughter owned the rope, my mother often told me, and the child never throve after, and used to be starting up out of her sleep, and screeching in the night-time, wid dhrames and frights that cum an her; and they said how it was the speerit of the ould Judge that was tormentin' her; and she used to be roaring and yelling out to hould back the big ould fellow with the crooked neck; and then she'd screech "Oh, the master! the master! he's stampin' at me, and beckoning to me! Mother, darling, don't let me go!" And so the poor crathure died at last, and the docthers said it was wather on the brain, for it was all they could say.'

'How long ago was all this?' I asked.

'Oh, then, how would I know?' she answered. 'But it must be a wondherful long time ago, for the housekeeper was an ould woman, with a pipe in her mouth, and not a tooth left, and better nor eighty years ould when my mother was first married; and they said she was a rale buxom, fine-dressed woman when the ould Judge come to his end; an', indeed, my mother's not far from eighty years ould herself this day; and what made it worse for the unnatural ould villain, God rest his soul, to frighten the little girl out of the world the way he did, was what was mostly thought and believed by every one. My mother says how the poor little crathure was his own child; for he was by all accounts an ould villain every way, an' the hangin'est judge that ever was known in Ireland's ground.'

'From what you said about the danger of sleeping in that bedroom,' said I, 'I suppose there were stories about the ghost having appeared there to others.'

'Well, there *was* things said—quare things, surely,' she answered, as it seemed, with some reluctance. 'And why would not there? Sure was it not up in that same room he slept for more than twenty years? and was it not in the *alcove* he got the rope ready that done his own business at last, the way he done many a betther man's in his lifetime?—and was not the body lying in the same bed after death, and put in the coffin there, too, and carried out to his grave from it in Pether's churchyard, after the coroner was done? But there was quare stories—my mother has them all—about how one Nicholas Spaight got into trouble on the head of it.'

'And what did they say of this Nicholas Spaight?' I asked.

'Oh, for that matther, it's soon told,' she answered.

And she certainly did relate a very strange story, which so piqued my curiosity, that I took occasion to visit the ancient lady, her mother, from whom I learned many very curious particulars. Indeed, I am tempted to tell the tale, but my fingers are weary, and I must defer it. But if you wish to hear it another time, I shall do my best.

When we had heard the strange tale I have *not* told you, we put one or two further questions to her about the alleged spectral visitations, to which the house had, ever since the death of the wicked old Judge, been subjected.

'No one ever had luck in it,' she told us. 'There was always cross accidents, sudden deaths, and short times in it. The first that tuck it was a family—I forget their name—but at any rate there was two young ladies and their papa. He was about sixty, and a stout healthy gentleman as you'd wish to see at that age. Well, he slept in that unlucky back bedroom; and, God between us an' harm! sure enough he was found dead one morning, half out of the bed, with his head as black as a sloe, and swelled like a puddin', hanging down near the floor. It was a fit, they said. He was as dead as a mackerel, and so *he* could not say what it was; but the ould people was all sure that it was nothing at all but the ould Judge, God bless us! that frightened him out of his senses and his life together.

'Some time after there was a rich old maiden lady took the house. I don't know which room *she* slept in, but she lived alone; and at any rate, one morning, the servants going down early to their work, found her sitting on the passage-stairs, shivering and talkin' to herself, quite mad; and never a word more could any of *them* or her friends get from her ever afterwards but, "Don't ask me to go, for I promised to wait for him." They never made out from her who it was she meant by *him*, but of course those that knew all about the ould house were at no loss for the meaning of all that happened to her.

'Then afterwards, when the house was let out in lodgings, there was Micky Byrne that took the same room, with his wife and three little children; and sure I heard Mrs Byrne myself telling how the children used to be lifted up in the bed at night, she could not see by what mains; and how they were starting and screeching every hour, just all as one as the housekeeper's little girl that died, till at last one night poor Micky had a dhrop in him, the way he used now and again; and what do you think in the middle of the night he thought he heard a noise on the stairs, and being in liquor, nothing less id do him but out he must go himself to see what was wrong. Well, after that, all she ever heard of him was himself sayin', "Oh, God!" and a tumble that shook the very house; and there, sure enough, he was lying on the lower stairs, under the lobby, with his neck smashed double undher him, where he was flung over the banisters.'

Then the handmaiden added—

'I'll go down to the lane, and send up Joe Gavvey to pack up the rest of the taythings, and bring all the things across to your new lodgings.'

And so we all sallied out together, each of us breathing more freely, I have no doubt, as we crossed that ill-omened threshold for the last time.

Now, I may add thus much, in compliance with the immemorial usage of the realm of fiction, which sees the hero not only through his adventures, but fairly out of the world. You must have perceived that what the flesh, blood, and bone hero of romance proper is to the   regular compounder of fiction, this old house of brick, wood, and mortar is to the humble recorder of this true tale. I, therefore, relate, as in duty bound, the catastrophe which ultimately befell it, which was simply this—that about two years subsequently to my story it was taken by a quack doctor, who called himself Baron Duhlstoerf, and filled the parlour windows with bottles of indescribable horrors preserved in brandy, and the newspapers with the usual grandiloquent and mendacious advertisements. This gentleman among his virtues did not reckon sobriety, and one night, being overcome with much wine, he set fire to his bed curtains, partially burned himself, and totally consumed the house. It was afterwards rebuilt, and for a time an undertaker established himself in the premises.

I have now told you my own and Tom's adventures, together with some valuable collateral particulars; and having acquitted myself of my engagement, I wish you a very good night, and pleasant dreams.

3

CHARLOTTE RIDDELL

The Last of Squire Ennismore

'Did I see it myself? No, sir; I did not see it; and my father before me did not see it; nor his father before him, and he was Phil Regan, just the same as myself. But it is true, for all that; just as true as that you are looking at the very place where the whole thing happened. My great-grandfather (and he did not die till he was ninety-eight) used to tell, many and many's the time, how he met the stranger, night after night, walking lonesome-like about the sands where most of the wreckage came ashore.'

'And the old house, then, stood behind that belt of Scotch firs?'

'Yes; and a fine house it was, too. Hearing so much talk about it when a boy, my father said, made him often feel as if he knew every room in the building, though it had all fallen to ruin before he was born. None of the family ever lived in it after the squire went away. Nobody else could be got to stop in the place. There used to be awful noises, as if something was being pitched from the top of the great staircase down in to the hall; and then there would be a sound as if a hundred people were clinking glasses and talking all together at once. And then it seemed as if barrels were rolling in the cellars; and there would be screeches, and howls, and laughing, fit to make your blood run cold. They say there is gold hid away in the cellars; but not one has ever ventured to find it. The very children won't come here to play; and when the men are ploughing the field behind, nothing will make them stay in it, once the day begins to change. When the night is coming on, and the tide creeps in on the sand, more than one thinks he has seen mighty queer things on the shore.'

'But what is it really they think they see? When I asked my land-lord to tell me the story from beginning to end, he said he could not remember it; and, at any rate, the whole rigmarole was non-sense, put together to please strangers.'

'And what is he but a stranger himself? And how should he know the doings of real quality like the Ennismores? For they were gentry, every one of them—good old stock; and as for wickedness, you might have searched Ireland through and not found their match. It is a sure thing, though, that if Riley can't tell you the story, I can; for, as I said, my own people were in it, of a manner of speak-ing. So, if your honour will rest yourself off your feet, on that bit of a bank, I'll set down my creel and give you the whole pedigree of how Squire Ennismore went away from Ardwinsagh.'

It was a lovely day, in the early part of June; and, as the English-man cast himself on a low ridge of sand, he looked over Ardwin-sagh Bay with a feeling of ineffable content. To his left lay the Purple Headland; to his right, a long range of breakers, that went straight out into the Atlantic till they were lost from sight; in front lay the Bay of Ardwinsagh, with its bluish-green water sparkling in the summer sunlight, and here and there breaking over some sunken rock, against which the waves spent themselves in foam.

'You see how the current's set, Sir? That is what makes it dan-gerous for them as doesn't know the coast, to bathe here at any time, or walk when the tide is flowing. Look how the sea is creep-ing in now, like a racehorse at the finish. It leaves that tongue of sand bars to the last, and then, before you could look round, it has you up to the middle. That is why I made bold to speak to you; for it is not alone on the account of Squire Ennismore the bay has a bad name. But it is about him and the old house you want to hear. The last mortal being that tried to live in it, my great-grandfather said, was a creature, by name Molly Leary; and she had neither kith nor kin, and begged for her bite and sup, sheltering herself at night in a turf cabin she had built at the back of a ditch. You may be sure she thought herself a made woman when the agent said, "Yes: she might try if she could stop in the house; there was peat and bog-wood," he told her, "and half-a-crown a week for the winter, and a golden guinea once Easter came," when the house was to be put in order for the family; and his wife gave Molly some warm clothes and a blanket or two; and she was well set up.

'You may be sure she didn't choose the worst room to sleep in; and for a while all went quiet, till one night she was wakened by feeling the bedstead lifted by the four corners and shaken like a carpet. It was a heavy four-post bedstead, with a solid top: and her life seemed to go out of her with the fear. If it had been a ship in a storm off the Headland, it couldn't have pitched worse and then, all of a sudden, it was dropped with such a bang as nearly drove the heart into her mouth.

'But that, she said, was nothing to the screaming and laughing, and hustling and rushing that filled the house. If a hundred people had been running hard along the passages and tumbling downstairs, they could not have made greater noise.

'Molly never was able to tell how she got clear of the place; but a man coming late home from Ballycloyne Fair found the creature crouched under the old thorn there, with very little on her—saving your honour's presence. She had a bad fever, and talked about strange things, and never was the same woman after.'

'But what was the beginning of all this? When did the house first get the name of being haunted?'

'After the old Squire went away: that was what I purposed telling you. He did not come here to live regularly till he had got well on in years. He was near seventy at the time I am talking about; but he held himself as upright as ever, and rode as hard as the youngest; and could have drunk a whole roomful under the table, and walked up to bed as unconcerned as you please at the dead of the night.

'He was a terrible man. You couldn't lay your tongue to a wickedness he had not been in the forefront of—drinking, duelling, gambling—all manner of sins had been meat and drink to him since he was a boy almost. But at last he did something in London so bad, so beyond the beyonds, that he thought he had best come home and live among people who did not know so much about his goings on as the English. It was said that he wanted to try and stay

31

in this world for ever; and that he had got some secret drops that kept him well and hearty. There was something wonderful queer about him, anyhow.

'He could hold foot with the youngest; and he was strong, and had a fine fresh colour in his face; and his eyes were like a hawk's; and there was not a break in his voice—and him near upon three-score and ten!

'At last and at long last it came to be the March before he was seventy—the worst March ever known in all these parts—such blowing, sleeting, snowing, had not been experienced in the memory of man; when one blusterous night some foreign vessel went to bits on the Purple Headland. They say it was an awful sound to hear the death-cry that went up high above the noise of the wind; and it was as bad a sight to see the shore there strewed with corpses of all sorts and sizes, from the little cabin-boy to the grizzled seaman.

'They never knew who they were or where they came from, but some of the men had crosses, and beads, and such like, so the priest said they belonged to him, and they were all buried deeply and decently in the chapel graveyard.

'There was not much wreckage of value drifted on shore. Most of what is lost about the Head stays there; but one thing did come into the bay—a puncheon of brandy.

'The Squire claimed it; it was his right to have all that came on his land, and he owned this sea-shore from the Head to the breakers—every foot—so, in course, he had the brandy; and there was sore ill will because he gave his men nothing, not even a glass of whiskey.

'Well, to make a long story short, that was the most wonderful liquor anybody ever tasted. The gentry came from far and near to take share, and it was cards and dice, and drinking and story-telling night after night—week in, week out. Even on Sundays, God forgive them! The officers would drive over from Ballycloyne, and sit emptying tumbler after tumbler till Monday morning came, for it made beautiful punch.

'But all at once people quit coming—a word went round that the liquor was not all it ought to be. Nobody could say what ailed it, but it got about that in some way men found it did not suit them.

'For one thing, they were losing money very fast.

'They could not make head against the Squire's luck, and a hint was dropped the puncheon ought to have been towed out to sea, and sunk in fifty fathoms of water.

'It was getting to the end of April, and fine, warm weather for the time of year, when first one and then another, and then another still, began to take notice of a stranger who walked the shore alone at night. He was a dark man, the same colour as the drowned crew lying in the chapel graveyard, and had rings in his ears, and wore a strange kind of hat, and cut wonderful antics as he walked, and had an ambling sort of gait, curious to look at. Many tried to talk to him, but he only shook his head; so, as nobody could make out where he came from or what he wanted, they made sure he was the spirit of some poor wretch who was tossing about the Head, longing for a snug corner in holy ground.

'The priest went and tried to get some sense out of him.

' "Is it Christian burial you're wanting?" asked his reverence; but the creature only shook his head.

' "Is it word sent the wives and daughters you've left orphans and widows, you'd like?" But no; it wasn't that.

' "Is it for sin committed you're doomed to walk this way? Would masses comfort ye? There's a heathen," said his reverence; "Did you ever hear tell of a Christian that shook his head when masses were mentioned?"

' "Perhaps he doesn't understand English, Father," says one of the officers who was there; "Try him with Latin."

'No sooner said than done. The priest started off with such a string of aves and paters that the stranger fairly took to his heels and ran.

' "He is an evil spirit," explained the priest, when he stopped, tired out, "and I have exorcized him."

'But next night my gentleman was back again, as unconcerned as ever.

' "And he'll just have to stay," said his reverence, "For I've got lumbago in the small of my back, and pains in all my joints—never to speak of a hoarseness with standing there shouting; and I don't believe he understood a sentence I said."

'Well, this went on for a while, and people got that frightened of the man, or appearance of a man, they would not go near the sand; till in the end, Squire Ennismore, who had always scoffed at the talk, took it into his head he would go down one night, and see into the rights of the matter. He, maybe, was feeling lonesome, because, as I told your honour before, people had left off coming to the house, and there was nobody for him to drink with.

'Out he goes, then, bold as brass; and there were a few followed him. The man came forward at sight of the Squire and took off his hat with a foreign flourish. Not to be behind in civility, the Squire lifted his.

' "I have come, sir," he said, speaking very loud, to try to make him understand, "to know if you are looking for anything, and whether I can assist you to find it."

'The man looked at the Squire as if he had taken the greatest liking to him, and took off his hat again.

' "Is it the vessel that was wrecked you are distressed about?"

'There came no answer, only a mournful shake of the head.

' "Well, *I* haven't your ship, you know; it went all to bits months ago; and, as for the sailors, they are snug and sound enough in consecrated ground."

'The man stood and looked at the Squire with a queer sort of smile on his face.

' "What *do* you want?" asked Mr Ennismore in a bit of a passion. "If anything belonging to you went down with the vessel, it's about the Head you ought to be looking for it, not here—unless, indeed, it's after the brandy you're fretting!"

'Now, the Squire had tried him in English and French, and was now speaking a language you'd have thought nobody could understand; but, faith, it seemed natural as kissing to the stranger.

' "Oh! That's where you are from, is it?" said the Squire. "Why couldn't you have told me so at once? I can't give you the brandy, because it mostly is drunk; but come along, and you shall have as stiff a glass of punch as ever crossed your lips." And without more to-do off they went, as sociable as you please, jabbering together in some outlandish tongue that made moderate folks' jaws ache to hear it.

'That was the first night they conversed together, but it wasn't the last. The stranger must have been the height of good company, for the Squire never tired of him. Every evening, regularly, he came up to the house, always dressed the same, always smiling and polite, and then the Squire called for brandy and hot water, and they drank and played cards till cock-crow, talking and laughing into the small hours.

'This went on for weeks and weeks, nobody knowing where the man came from, or where he went; only two things the old house-keeper did know—that the puncheon was nearly empty, and that the Squire's flesh was wasting off him; and she felt so uneasy she went to the priest, but he could give her no manner of comfort.

'She got so concerned at last that she felt bound to listen at the dining-room door; but they always talked in that foreign gibberish, and whether it was blessing or cursing they were at she couldn't tell.

'Well, the upshot of it came one night in July—on the eve of the Squire's birthday—there wasn't a drop of spirit left in the puncheon—no, not as much as would drown a fly. They had drunk the whole lot clean up—and the old woman stood trembling, expecting every minute to hear the bell ring for more brandy, for where was she to get more if they wanted any?

'All at once the Squire and the stranger came out into the hall. It was a full moon, and light as day.

' "I'll go home with you tonight by way of a change," says the Squire.

' "Will you so?" asked the other.

' "That I will," answered the Squire.

' "It is your own choice, you know."

' "Yes; it is my own choice; let us go."

'So they went. And the housekeeper ran up to the window on the great staircase and watched the way they took. Her niece lived there as housemaid, and she came and watched, too; and, after a while, the butler as well. They all turned their faces this way, and looked after their master walking beside the strange man along these very sands. Well, they saw them walk on, and on, and on, and on, till the water took them to their knees, and then to their waists, and then to their arm-pits, and then to their throats and their heads; but long before that the women and the butler were running out on the shore as fast as they could, shouting for help.'

'Well?' said the Englishman.

'Living or dead, Squire Ennismore never came back again. Next morning, when the tides ebbed again, one walking over the sand saw the print of a cloven foot—that he tracked to the water's edge. Then everybody knew where the Squire had gone, and with whom.'

'And no more search was made?'

'Where would have been the use searching?'

'Not much, I suppose. It's a strange story, anyhow.'

'But true, your honour—every word of it.'

'Oh! I have no doubt of that,' was the satisfactory reply.

4

ROSA MULHOLLAND

The Ghost at the Rath

Many may disbelieve this story, yet there are some still living who can remember hearing, when children, of the events which it details, and of the strange sensation which their publicity excited. The tale, in its present form, is copied, by permission, from a memoir written by the chief actor in the romance, and preserved as a sort of heirloom in the family whom it concerns.

In the year —— I, John Thunder, Captain in the —— Regiment, having passed many years abroad following my profession, received notice that I had become owner of certain properties which I had never thought to inherit. I set off for my native land, arrived in Dublin, found that my good fortune was real, and at once began to look about me for old friends. The first I met with, quite by accident, was curly-headed Frank O'Brien, who had been at school with me, though I was ten years his senior. He was curly-headed still, and handsome, as he had promised to be, but careworn and poor. During an evening spent at his chambers I drew all his history from him. He was a briefless barrister. As a man he was not more talented than he had been as a boy. Hard work and anxiety had not brought him success, only broken his health and soured his mind. He was in love, and he could not marry. I soon knew all about Mary Leonard, his fiancée, whom he had met at a house in the country somewhere, in which she was governess. They had now been engaged for two years—she active and hopeful, he sick and despondent. From the letters of hers which he showed me, I thought she was worth all the devotion he felt for her. I considered a good deal about what could be done for Frank, but I could not easily hit upon a plan to assist him. For ten chances you have of helping a sharp man, you have not two for a dull one.

In the meantime my friend must regain his health, and a change of air and scene was necessary. I urged him to make a voyage of discovery to the Rath, an old house and park which had come into my possession as portion of my recently acquired estates. I had never been to the place myself; but it had once been the residence of Sir Luke Thunder, of generous memory, and I knew that it was furnished, and provided with a caretaker. I pressed him to leave Dublin at once, and promised to follow him as soon as I found it possible to do so.

So Frank went down to the Rath. The place was two hundred miles away; he was a stranger there, and far from well. When the first week came to an end, and I had heard nothing from him, I did not like the silence; when a fortnight had passed, and still not a word to say he was alive, I felt decidedly uncomfortable; and when the third week of his absence arrived at Saturday without bringing me news, I found myself whizzing through a part of the country I had never travelled before, in the same train in which I had seen Frank seated at our parting.

I reached D——, and, shouldering my knapsack, walked right into the heart of a lovely woody country. Following the directions I had received, I made my way to a lonely road, on which I met not a soul, and which seemed cut out of the heart of a forest, so closely were the trees ranked on either side, and so dense was the twilight made by the meeting and intertwining of the thick branches overhead. In these shades I came upon a gate, like a gate run to seed, with tall, thin, brick pillars, brandishing long grasses from their heads, and spotted with a melancholy crust of creeping moss. I jangled a cracked bell, and an old man appeared from the thickets within, stared at me, then admitted me with a rusty key. I breathed freely on hearing that my friend was well and to be seen. I presented a letter to the old man, having a fancy not to avow myself.

I found my friend walking up and down the alleys of a neglected orchard, with the lichened branches tangled above his head, and ripe apples rotting about his feet. His hands were locked behind his back, and his head was set on one side, listening to the singing of a bird. I never had seen him look so well; yet there was a vacancy about his whole air which I did not like. He did not seem at all surprised to see me, asked had he really not written to me; thought he had; was so comfortable that he had forgotten everything else. He fancied he had only been there about three days; could not imagine how the time had passed. He seemed to talk wildly, and this, coupled with the unusual happy placidity of his manner, confounded me. The place knew him, he told me confidentially; the place belonged to him, or should; the birds sang him this, the very trees bent before him as he passed, the air whispered him that he had been long expected, and should be poor no more. Wrestling with my judgement ere it might pronounce him mad, I followed him indoors. The Rath was no ordinary old country-house. The acres around it were so wildly overgrown that it was hard to decide which had been pleasure-ground and where the thickets had begun. The plan of the house was fine, with mullioned windows, and here and there a fleck of stained glass flinging back the challenge of an angry sunset. The vast rooms were full of a dusky glare from the sky as I strolled through them in the twilight. The antique furniture had many a blood-red stain on the abrupt notches of its dark carvings; the dusty mirrors flared back at the windows, while the faded curtains produced streaks of uncertain colour from the depths of their sullen foldings.

Dinner was laid for us in the library, a long wainscoted room, with an enormous fire roaring up the chimney, sending a dancing light over the dingy titles of long unopened books. The old man who had unlocked the gate for me served us at table, and, after drawing the dusty curtains, and furnishing us with a plentiful supply of fuel and wine, left us. His clanking hobnailed shoes went echoing away in the distance over the unmatted tiles of the vacant hall till a door closed with a resounding clang very far away, letting us know that we were shut up together for the night in this vast, mouldy, oppressive old house.

I felt as if I could scarcely breathe in it. I could not eat with my usual appetite. The air of the place seemed heavy and tainted.

I grew sick and restless. The very wine tasted badly, as if it had been drugged. I had a strange feeling that I had been in the house before, and that something evil had happened to me in it. Yet such could not be the case. What puzzled me most was, that I should feel dissatisfied at seeing Frank looking so well, and eating so heartily. A little time before I should have been glad to suffer something to see him as he looked now; and yet not quite as he looked now. There was a drowsy contentment about him which I could not understand. He did not talk of his work, or of any wish to return to it. He seemed to have no thought of anything but the delight of hanging about that old house, which had certainly cast a spell over him.

About midnight he seized a light, and proposed retiring to our rooms. 'I have such delightful dreams in this place,' he said. He volunteered, as we issued into the hall, to take me upstairs and show me the upper regions of his paradise. I said, 'Not tonight.' I felt a strange creeping sensation as I looked up the vast black staircase, wide enough for a coach to drive down, and at the heavy darkness bending over it like a curse, while our lamps made drips of light down the first two or three gloomy steps. Our bedrooms were on the ground floor, and stood opposite one another off a passage which led to a garden. Into mine Frank conducted me, and left me for his own.

The uneasy feeling which I have described did not go from me with him, and I felt a restlessness amounting to pain when left alone in my chamber. Efforts had evidently been made to render the room habitable, but there was a something antagonistic to sleep in every angle of its many crooked corners. I kicked chairs out of their prim order along the wall, and banged things about here and there; finally, thinking that a good night's rest was the best cure for an inexplicably disturbed frame of mind, I undressed as quickly as possible, and laid my head on my pillow under a canopy, like the wings of a gigantic bird of prey wheeling above me ready to pounce.

But I could not sleep. The wind grumbled in the chimney, and the boughs swished in the garden outside; and between these noises I thought I heard sounds coming from the interior of the old house, where all should have been still as the dead down in their vaults. I could not make out what these sounds were. Sometimes I thought I heard feet running about, sometimes I could have sworn there were double knocks, tremendous tantarararas at the great hall door. Sometimes I heard the clashing of dishes, the echo of voices calling, and the dragging about of furniture. Whilst I sat up in bed trying to account for these noises, my door suddenly flew open, a bright light streamed in from the passage without, and a powdered servant in an elaborate livery of antique pattern stood holding the handle of the door in his hand, and bowing low to me in the bed.

'Her ladyship, my mistress, desires your presence in the drawing-room, sir.'

This was announced in the measured tone of a well-trained domestic. Then with another bow he retired, the door closed, and I was left in the dark to determine whether I had not suddenly awakened from a tantalizing dream. In spite of my very wakeful sensations, I believe I should have endeavoured to convince myself that I had been sleeping, but that I perceived light shining under my door, and through the keyhole, from the passage. I got up, lit my lamp, and dressed myself as hastily as I was able.

I opened my door, and the passage down which a short time before I had almost groped my way, with my lamp blinking in the dense foggy darkness, was now illuminated with a light as bright as gas. I walked along it quickly, looking right and left to see whence the glare proceeded. Arriving at the hall, I found it also blazing with light, and filled with perfume. Groups of choice plants, heavy with blossoms, made it look like a garden. The mosaic floor was strewn with costly mats. Soft colours and gilding shone from the walls, and canvases that had been black gave forth faces of men and women looking brightly from their burnished frames. Servants were running about, the dining-room and drawing-room doors were opening and shutting, and as I looked through each I saw vistas of light and colour, the moving of brilliant crowds, the waving of feathers, and glancing of brilliant dresses and uniforms. A festive hum reached me with a drowsy subdued sound, as if I were

41

listening with stuffed ears. Standing aside by an orange tree, I gave up speculating on what this might be, and concentrated all my powers on observation.

Wheels were heard suddenly, and a resounding knock banged at the door till it seemed that the very rooks in the chimneys must be startled out of their nests. The door flew open, a flaming of lanterns was seen outside, and a dazzling lady came up the steps and swept into the hall. When she held up her cloth of silver train, I could see the diamonds that twinkled on her feet. Her bosom was covered with roses, and there was a red light in her eyes like the reflection from a hundred glowing fires. Her black hair went coiling about her head, and couched among the braids lay a jewel not unlike the head of a snake. She was flashing and glowing with gems and flowers. Her beauty and brilliance made me dizzy. Then came a faintness in the air, as if her breath had poisoned it. A whirl of storm came in with her, and rushed up the staircase like a moan. The plants shuddered and shed their blossoms, and all the lights grew dim a moment, then flared up again.

Now the drawing-room door opened, and a gentleman came out with a young girl leaning on his arm. He was a fine-looking, middle-aged gentleman, with a mild countenance.

The girl was a slender creature, with golden hair and a pale face. She was dressed in pure white, with a large ruby like a drop of blood at her throat. They advanced together to receive the lady who had arrived. The gentleman offered his arm to the stranger, and the girl who was displaced for her fell back, and walked behind them with a downcast air. I felt irresistibly impelled to follow them, and passed with them into the drawing-room. Never had I mixed in a finer, gayer crowd. The costumes were rich and of an old-fashioned pattern. Dancing was going forward with spirit— minuets and country dances. The stately gentleman was evidently the host, and moved among the company, introducing the magnificent lady right and left. He led her to the head of the room presently, and they mixed in the dance. The arrogance of her manner and the fascination of her beauty were wonderful.

I cannot attempt to describe the strange manner in which I was in this company, and yet not of it. I seemed to view all I beheld through some fine and subtle medium. I saw clearly, yet I felt that it was not with my ordinary naked eyesight. I can compare it to nothing but looking at a scene through a piece of smoked or coloured glass. And just in the same way (as I have said before) all sounds seemed to reach me as if I were listening with ears imperfectly stuffed. No one present took any notice of me. I spoke to several, and they made no reply—did not even turn their eyes upon me, nor show in any way that they heard me. I planted myself straight in the way of a fine fellow in a general's uniform, but he, swerving neither to right nor left by an inch, kept on his way, as though I were a streak of mist, and left me behind him. Everyone I touched eluded me somehow. Substantial as they all looked, I could not contrive to lay my hand on anything that felt like solid flesh. Two or three times I felt a momentary relief from the oppressive sensations which distracted me, when I firmly believed I saw Frank's head at some distance among the crowd, now in one room and now in another, and again in the conservatory, which was hung with lamps, and filled with people walking about among the flowers. But, whenever I approached, he had vanished. At last I came upon him, sitting by himself on a couch behind a curtain watching the dancers. I laid my hand upon his shoulder. Here was something substantial at last. He did not look up; he seemed aware neither of my touch nor my speech. I looked in his staring eyes, and found that he was sound asleep. I could not wake him.

Curiosity would not let me remain by his side. I again mixed with the crowd, and found the stately host still leading about the magnificent lady. No one seemed to notice that the golden-haired girl was sitting weeping in a corner; no one but the beauty in the silver train, who sometimes glanced at her contemptuously. Whilst I watched her distress a group came between me and her, and I wandered into another room, where, as though I had turned from one picture of her to look at another, I beheld her dancing gaily, in the full glee of Sir Roger de Coverley, with a fine-looking youth, who was more plainly dressed than any other person in the room. Never was a better-matched pair to look at. Down the middle they danced, hand in hand, his face full of tenderness, hers beaming with joy, right and left bowing and curtseying, parted and meeting again, smiling and whispering; but over the heads of smaller women there were the fierce eyes of the magnificent beauty scowling at them. Then again the crowd shifted around me, and this scene was lost.

For some time I could see no trace of the golden-haired girl in any of the rooms. I looked for her in vain, till at last I caught a glimpse of her standing smiling in a doorway with her finger lifted, beckoning. At whom? Could it be at me? Her eyes were fixed on mine. I hastened into the hall, and caught sight of her white dress passing up the wide black staircase from which I had shrunk some hours earlier. I followed her, she keeping some steps in advance. It was intensely dark, but by the gleaming of her gown I was able to trace her flying figure. Where we went I knew not, up how many stairs, down how many passages, till we arrived at a low-roofed large room with sloping roof and queer windows where there was a dim light, like the sanctuary light in a deserted church. Here, when I entered, the golden head was glimmering over something which I presently discerned to be a cradle wrapped round with white curtains, and with a few fresh flowers fastened up on the hood of it, as if to catch a baby's eye. The fair sweet face looked up at me with a glow of pride on it, smiling with happy dimples. The white hands unfolded the curtains, and stripped back the coverlet. Then, suddenly there went a rushing moan all round the weird room, that seemed like a gust of wind forcing in through the crannies, and shaking the jingling old windows in their sockets. The cradle was an empty one. The girl fell back with a look of horror on her pale face that I shall never forget, then, flinging her arms above her head, she dashed from the room.

I followed her as fast as I was able, but the wild white figure was too swift for me. I had lost her before I reached the bottom of the staircase. I searched for her, first in one room, then in another, neither could I see her foe (as I already believed to be), the lady of the silver train. At length I found myself in a small ante-room, where a lamp was expiring on the table. A window was open, close by it the golden-haired girl was lying sobbing in a chair, while the magnificent lady was bending over her as if soothingly, and offering her something to drink in a goblet. The moon was rising behind the two figures. The shuddering light of the lamp was flickering over the girl's bright head, the rich embossing of the golden cup, the lady's silver robes, and, I thought, the jewelled eyes of the serpent looked out from her bending head. As I watched, the girl raised her face and drank, then suddenly dashed the goblet away; while a cry such as I never heard but once, and shiver to remember, rose to the very roof of the old house, and the clear sharp word '*Poisoned!*' rang and reverberated from hall and chamber in a thousand echoes, like the clash of a peal of bells. The girl dashed herself from the open window, leaving the cry clamouring behind her. I heard the violent opening of doors and running of feet, but I waited for nothing more. Maddened by what I had witnessed, I would have felled the murderess, but she glided unhurt from under my vain blow. I sprang from the window after the wretched white figure. I saw it flying on before me with a speed I could not overtake. I ran till I was dizzy. I called like a madman, and heard the owls croaking back to me. The moon grew huge and bright, the trees grew out before it like the bushy heads of giants, the river lay keen and shining like a long unsheathed sword, couching for deadly work among the rushes. The white figure shimmered and vanished, glittered brightly on before me, shimmered and vanished again, shimmered, staggered, fell, and disappeared in the river. Of what she was, phantom or reality, I thought not at the moment; she had the semblance of a human being going to destruction, and I had the frenzied impulse to save her. I rushed forward with one last effort, struck my foot against the root of a tree, and was dashed to the ground. I remember a crash, momentary pain and confusion; then nothing more.

When my senses returned, the red clouds of the dawn were shining in the river beside me. I arose to my feet, and found that, though much bruised, I was otherwise unhurt. I busied my mind in recalling the strange circumstances which had brought me to that place in the dead of the night. The recollection of all I had witnessed was vividly present to my mind. I took my way slowly to the house, almost expecting to see the marks of wheels and other indications of last night's revel, but the rank grass that covered the gravel was uncrushed, not a blade disturbed, not a stone displaced. I shook one of the drawing-room windows till I shook off the old rusty hasp inside, flung up the creaking sash, and entered. Where were the brilliant draperies and carpets, the soft gilding, the vases teeming with flowers, the thousand sweet odours of the night before? Not a trace of them; no, nor even a ragged cobweb swept away, nor a stiff chair moved an inch from its melancholy place, nor the face of a mirror relieved from one speck of its obscuring dust!

Coming back into the open air, I met the old man from the gate walking up one of the weedy paths. He eyed me meaningly from head to foot, but I gave him good-morrow cheerfully.

'You see I am poking about early,' I said.

'I'faith, sir,' said he, 'an' ye look like a man that had been pokin' about *all night.*'

'How so?' said I.

'Why, ye see, sir,' said he, 'I'm used to 't, an' I can read it in yer face like prent. Some sees one thing an' some another, an' some only feels an' hears. The poor jintleman inside, *he* says nothin', but he has beautyful dhrames. An' for the Lord's sake, sir, take him out o' this, for I've seen him wandherin' about like a ghost himself in the heart of the night, an' him that sound sleepin' that I couldn't wake him!'

At breakfast I said nothing to Frank of my strange adventures. He had rested well, he said, and boasted of his enchanting dreams. I asked him to describe them, when he grew perplexed and annoyed. He remembered nothing, but that his spirit had been delightfully entertained whilst his body reposed. I now felt a curiosity to go through the old house, and was not surprised, on pushing open a door at the end of a remote mouldy passage, to enter the identical chamber into which I had followed the pale-faced girl when she beckoned me out of the drawing-room. There were the low brooding roof and slanting walls, the short wide latticed windows to which the noonday sun was trying to pierce through a forest of leaves. The hangings rotting with age shook like dreary banners at the opening of the door, and there in the middle of the room was the cradle; only the curtains that had been white were blackened with dirt, and laced and overlaced with cobwebs. I parted the curtains, bringing down a shower of dust upon the floor, and saw lying upon the pillow, within, a child's tiny shoe, and a toy. I need not describe the rest of the house. It was vast and rambling, and, as far as furniture and decorations were concerned, the wreck of grandeur.

Having strange subject for meditation, I walked alone in the orchard that evening. This orchard sloped towards the river I have mentioned before. The trees were old and stunted, and the branches tangled overhead. The ripe apples were rolling in the long bleached grass. A row of taller trees, sycamores and chestnuts, straggled along by the river's edge, ferns and tall weeds grew round and amongst them, and between their trunks, and behind the rifts in the foliage, the water was seen to flow. Walking up and down one of the paths I alternately faced these trees and turned my back upon them. Once when coming towards them I chanced to lift my glance, started, drew my hands across my eyes, looked again, and finally stood still gazing in much astonishment. I saw distinctly the figure of a lady standing by one of the trees, bending low towards the grass. Her face was a little turned away, her dress a bluish-white, her mantle a dun-brown colour. She held a spade in her hand, and her foot was upon it, as if she were in the act of digging. I gazed at her for some time, vainly trying to guess at whom she might be, then I advanced towards her. As I approached, the outlines of her figure broke up and disappeared, and I found that she was only an illusion presented to me by the curious accidental grouping of the lines of two trees which had shaped the space between them into the semblance of the form I have described. A patch of the flowing water had been her robe, a piece of russet moorland her cloak. The spade was an awkward young shoot slanting up from the root of one of the trees. I stepped back and tried to piece her out again bit by bit, but could not succeed.

That night I did not feel at all inclined to return to my dismal chamber, and lie awaiting such another summons as I had once received. When Frank bade me good-night, I heaped fresh coals on the fire, took down from the shelves a book, from which I lifted the dust in layers with my penknife, and, dragging an armchair close to the hearth, tried to make myself as comfortable as might be. I am a strong, robust man, very unimaginative, and little troubled with affections of the nerves, but I confess that my feelings were not enviable, sitting thus alone in that queer old house, with last night's strange pantomime still vividly present to my memory. In spite of my efforts at coolness, I was excited by the prospect of what yet might be in store for me before morning. But these feelings passed away as the night wore on, and I nodded asleep over my book.

I was startled by the sound of a brisk light step walking overhead. Wide awake at once, I sat up and listened. The ceiling was low, but I could not call to mind what room it was that lay above the library in which I sat. Presently I heard the same step upon the stairs, and the loud sharp rustling of a silk dress sweeping against the banisters. The step paused at the library door, and then there was silence. I got up, and with all the courage I could summon seized a light, and opened the door; but there was nothing in the hall but the usual heavy darkness and damp mouldy air. I confess I felt more uncomfortable at that moment than I had done at any time during the preceding night. All the visions that had then appeared to me had produced nothing like the horror of thus feeling a supernatural presence which my eyes were not permitted to behold.

I returned to the library, and passed the night there. Next day I sought for the room above it in which I had heard the footsteps, but could discover no entrance to any such room. Its windows, indeed, I counted from the outside, though they were so overgrown with ivy I could hardly discern them, but in the interior of the house I could find no door to the chamber. I asked Frank about it, but he knew and cared nothing on the subject; I asked the old man at the lodge, and he shook his head.

'Och!' he said, 'don't ask about that room. The door's built up, and flesh and blood have no consarn wid it. It was *her own* room.'

'Whose own?' I asked.

'Ould Lady Thunder's. An' whist, sir! *that's her grave!*'

'What do you mean?' I said. 'Are you out of your mind?'

He laughed queerly, drew nearer, and lowered his voice. 'Nobody has asked about the room these years but yourself,' he said. 'Nobody misses it goin' over the house. My grandfather was an old retainer o' the Thunder family, my father was in the service too, an' I was born myself before the ould lady died. Yon was her room, an' she left her eternal curse on her family if so be they didn't lave her coffin there. *She* wasn't goin' undher the ground to the worms. So there it was left, an' they built up the door. God love ye, sir, an' don't go near it. I wouldn't have told you, only I know ye've seen plenty about already, an' ye have the look o' one that'd be ferretin' things out, savin' yer presence.'

He looked at me knowingly, but I gave him no information, only thanked him for putting me on my guard. I could scarcely credit what he told me about the room; but my curiosity was excited regarding it. I made up my mind that day to try and induce Frank to quit the place on the morrow. I felt more and more convinced that the atmosphere was not healthful for his mind, whatever it might be for his body. The sooner we left the spot the better for us both; but the remaining night which I had to pass there I resolved on devoting to the exploring of the walled-up chamber. What impelled me to this resolve I do not know. The undertaking was not a pleasant one, and I should hardly have ventured on it had I been forced to remain much longer at the Rath. But I knew there was little chance of sleep for me in that house, and I thought I might as well go and seek for my adventures as sit waiting for them to come for me, as I had done the night before. I felt a relish for my enterprise, and expected the night with satisfaction. I did not say anything of my intention either to Frank or the old man at the lodge. I did not want to make a fuss, and have my doings talked of all over the country. I may as well mention here that again, on this evening, when walking in the orchard, I saw the figure of the lady digging between the trees. And again I saw that this figure was an illusive appearance; that the water was her gown, and the moorland her cloak, and a willow in the distance her tresses.

As soon as the night was pretty far advanced, I placed a ladder against the window which was least covered over with the ivy, and mounted it, having provided myself with a dark lantern. The moon rose full behind some trees that stood like a black bank against the horizon, and glimmered on the panes as I ripped away branches and leaves with a knife, and shook the old crazy casement open. The sashes were rotten, and the fastenings easily gave way. I placed my lantern on a bench within, and was soon standing beside it in the chamber. The air was insufferably close and mouldy, and I flung the window open to the widest, and beat the bowering ivy still further back from about it, so as to let the fresh air of heaven blow into the place. I then took my lantern in hand, and began to look about me.

The room was vast and double; a velvet curtain hung between me and an inner chamber. The darkness was thick and irksome, and the scanty light of my lantern only tantalized me. My eyes fell on some tall spectral-looking candelabra furnished with wax candles, which, though black with age, still bore the marks of having been guttered by a draught that had blown on them fifty years ago. I lighted these; they burned up with a ghastly flickering, and the apartment, with its fittings, was revealed to me. These latter had been splendid in the days of their freshness: the appointments of the rest of the house were mean in comparison. The ceiling was painted with fine allegorical figures, also spaces of the walls between the dim mirrors and the sumptuous hangings of crimson velvet, with their tarnished golden tassels and fringes. The carpet still felt luxurious to the tread, and the dust could not altogether obliterate the elaborate fancy of its flowery design. There were gorgeous cabinets laden with curiosities, wonderfully carved chairs, rare vases, and antique glasses of every description, under some of which lay little heaps of dust which had once no doubt been blooming flowers. There was a table laden with books of poetry and science, drawings and drawing materials, which showed that the occupant of the room had been a person of mind. There was also a writing-table scattered over with yellow papers, and a work-table at a window, on which lay reels, a thimble, and a piece of what had once been white muslin, but was now saffron colour, sewn with gold thread, a rusty needle sticking in it. This and the pen lying on the inkstand, the paper-knife between the leaves of a book, the loose sketches shaken out by the side of a portfolio, and the ashes of a fire on the wide mildewed hearth-place, all suggested that the owner of this retreat had been snatched from it without warning, and that whoever had thought proper to build up the doors, had also thought proper to touch nothing that had belonged to her.

Having surveyed all these things, I entered the inner room, which was a bedroom. The furniture of this was in keeping with that of the other chamber. I saw dimly a bed enveloped in lace, and a dressing-table fancifully garnished and draped. Here I espied more candelabra, and going forward to set the lights burning, I stumbled against something. I turned the blaze of my lantern on this something, and started with a sudden thrill of horror. It was a large stone coffin.

I own that I felt very strangely for the next few minutes. When I had recovered the shock, I set the wax candles burning, and took a better survey of this odd burial-place. A wardrobe stood open, and I saw dresses hanging within. A gown lay upon a chair, as if just thrown off, and a pair of dainty slippers were beside it. The toilet-table looked as if only used yesterday, judging by the litter that covered it; hairbrushes lying this way and that way, essence-bottles with the stoppers out, paint pots uncovered, a ring here, a wreath of artificial flowers there, and in front of all that the coffin, the tarnished Cupids that bore the mirror between their hands smirking down at it with a grim complacency.

On the corner of this table was a small golden salver, holding a plate of some black mouldered food, an antique decanter filled with wine, a glass, and a phial with some thick black liquid, uncorked. I felt weak and sick with the atmosphere of the place, and I seized the decanter, wiped the dust from it with my handkerchief, tasted, found that the wine was good, and drank a moderate draught. Immediately it was swallowed I felt a horrid giddiness, and sank upon the coffin. A raging pain was in my head and a sense of suffocation in my chest. After a few intolerable moments I felt better, but the heavy air pressed on me stiflingly, and I rushed from this inner room into the larger and outer chamber. Here a blast of cool air revived me, and I saw that the place was changed.

A dozen other candelabra besides those I had lighted were flaming round the walls, the hearth was all ruddy with a blazing fire, everything that had been dim was bright, the lustre had returned to the gilding, the flowers bloomed in the vases. A lady was sitting before the hearth in a low armchair. Her light loose gown swept about her on the carpet, her black hair fell round her to her knees, and into it her hands were thrust as she leaned her forehead upon them, and stared between them into the fire. I had scarcely time to observe her attitude when she turned her head quickly towards me, and I recognized the handsome face of the magnificent lady who had played such a sinister part in the strange scenes that had been enacted before me two nights ago. I saw something dark looming behind her chair, but I thought it was only her shadow thrown backward by the firelight.

She arose and came to meet me, and I recoiled from her. There was something horridly fixed and hollow in her gaze, and filmy in the stirring of her garments. The shadow, as she moved, grew more firm and distinct in outline, and followed her like a servant where she went.

She crossed half of the room, then beckoned me, and sat down at the writing-table. The shadow waited beside her, adjusted her paper, placed the ink-bottle near her and the pen between her fingers. I felt impelled to approach her, and to take my place at her left shoulder, so as to be able to see what she might write. The shadow stood motionless at her other hand. As I became accustomed to the shadow's presence he grew more visibly loathsome and hideous. He was quite distinct from the lady, and moved independently of her with long ugly limbs. She hesitated about beginning to write, and he made a wild gesture with his arm, which brought her hand quickly to the paper, and her pen began to move at once. I needed not to bend and scrutinize in order to read. Every word as it was forming flashed before me like a meteor.

'I am the spirit of Madeline, Lady Thunder, who lived and died in this house, and whose coffin stands in yonder room among the vanities in which I delighted. I am constrained to make my confession to you, John Thunder, who are the present owner of the estates of your family.'

Here the hand trembled and stopped writing. But the shadow made a threatening gesture, and the hand fluttered on.

'I was beautiful, poor, and ambitious, and when I entered this house first on the night of a ball given by Sir Luke Thunder, I determined to become its mistress. His daughter, Mary Thunder, was the only obstacle in my way. She divined my intention, and stood between me and her father. She was a gentle, delicate girl, and no match for me. I pushed her aside, and became Lady Thunder. After that I hated her, and made her dread me. I had gained the object of my ambition, but I was jealous of the influence possessed by her over her father, and I revenged myself by crushing the joy out of her young life. In this I defeated my own purpose. She eloped with a young man who was devoted to her, though poor, and beneath her in station. Her father was indignant at first, and my malice was satisfied; but as time passed on I had no children, and she had a son, soon after whose birth her husband died. Then her father took her back to his heart, and the boy was his idol and heir.'

Again the hand stopped writing, the ghostly head drooped, and the whole figure was convulsed. But the shadow gesticulated fiercely, and, cowering under its menace, the wretched spirit went on:

'I caused the child to be stolen away. I thought I had done it cunningly, but she tracked the crime home to me. She came and accused me of it, and in the desperation of my terror at discovery, I gave her poison to drink. She rushed from me and from the house in frenzy, and in her mortal anguish fell in the river. People thought she had gone mad from grief for her child, and committed suicide.

I only knew the horrible truth. Sorrow brought an illness upon her father, of which he died. Up to the day of his death he had search made for the child. Believing that it was alive, and must be found, he willed all his property to it, his rightful heir, and to its heirs for ever. I buried the deeds under a tree in the orchard, and forged a will, in which all was bequeathed to me during my lifetime. I enjoyed my state and grandeur till the day of my death, which came upon me miserably, and, after that, my husband's possessions went to a distant relation of his family. Nothing more was heard of the fate of the child who was stolen; but he lived and married, and his daughter now toils for her bread—his daughter, who is the rightful owner of all that is said to belong to you, John Thunder. I tell you this that you may devote yourself to the task of discovering this wronged girl, and giving up to her that which you are unlawfully possessed of. Under the thirteenth tree standing on the brink of the river at the foot of the orchard you will find buried the genuine will of Sir Luke Thunder. When you have found and read it, do justice, as you value your soul. In order that you may know the grandchild of Mary Thunder when you find her, you shall behold her in a vision——'

The last words grew dim before me; the lights faded away, and all the place was in darkness, except one spot on the opposite wall. On this spot the light glimmered softly, and against the brightness the outlines of a figure appeared, faintly at first, but, growing firm and distinct, became filled in and rounded at last to the perfect semblance of life. The figure was that of a young girl in a plain black dress, with a bright, happy face, and pale gold hair softly banded on her fair forehead. She might have been the twin-sister of the pale-faced girl whom I had seen bending over the cradle two nights ago; but her healthier, gladder, and prettier sister. When I had gazed on her some moments, the vision faded away as it had come; the last vestige of the brightness died out upon the wall, and I found myself once more in total darkness. Stunned for a time by the sudden changes, I stood watching for the return of the lights and figures; but in vain. By and by my eyes grew accustomed to the obscurity, and I saw the sky glimmering behind the little window which I had left open. I could soon discern the writing-table beside me, and possessed myself of the slips of loose paper which lay upon it. I then made my way to the window. The first streaks of dawn were in the sky as I descended my ladder, and I thanked God that I breathed the fresh morning air once more, and heard the cheering sound of the cocks crowing.

All thought of acting immediately upon last night's strange revelations, almost all memory of them, was for the time banished from my mind by the unexpected trouble of the next few days. That morning I found an alarming change in Frank. Feeling sure that he was going to be ill, I engaged a lodging in a cottage in the neighbourhood, whither we removed before nightfall, leaving the accursed Rath behind us. Before midnight he was in the delirium of a raging fever.

I thought it right to let his poor little fiancée know his state, and wrote to her, trying to alarm her no more than was necessary. On the evening of the third day after my letter went I was sitting by Frank's bedside, when an unusual bustle outside aroused my curiosity, and going into the cottage kitchen I saw a figure standing in the firelight which seemed a third appearance of that vision of the pale-faced golden-haired girl which was now thoroughly imprinted on my memory—a third, with all the woe of the first and all the beauty of the second. But this was a living, breathing apparition. She was throwing off her bonnet and shawl, and stood there at home in a moment in her plain black dress. I drew my hand across my eyes to make sure that they did not deceive me. I had beheld so many supernatural visions lately that it seemed as though I could scarcely believe in the reality of anything till I had touched it.

'Oh, sir,' said the visitor, 'I am Mary Leonard, and are you poor Frank's friend? Oh, sir, we are all the world to one another, and I could not let him die without coming to see him!'

And here the poor little traveller burst into tears. I cheered her as well as I could, telling her that Frank would soon, I trusted, be out of all danger. She told me that she had thrown up her situation in order to come and nurse him. I said we had got a more experienced nurse than she could be, and then I gave her to the care of our landlady, a motherly countrywoman. After that I went back to Frank's bedside, nor left it for long till he was convalescent. The fever had swept away all that strangeness in his manner which had afflicted me, and he was quite himself again.

There was a joyful meeting of the lovers. The more I saw of Mary Leonard's bright face the more thoroughly was I convinced that she was the living counterpart of the vision I had seen in the burial chamber. I made enquiries as to her birth, and her father's history, and found that she was indeed the grandchild of that Mary Thunder whose history had been so strangely related to me, and the rightful heiress of all those properties which for a few months only had been mine. Under the tree in the orchard, the thirteenth, and that by which I had seen the lady digging, were found the buried deeds which had been described to me. I made an immediate transfer of property, whereupon some others who thought they had a chance of being my heirs disputed the matter with me, and went to law. Thus the affair has gained publicity, and become a nine days' wonder. Many things have been in my favour, however: the proving of Mary's birth and of Sir Luke's will, the identification of Lady Thunder's handwriting on the slips of paper which I had brought from the burial chamber; also other matters which a search in that chamber brought to light. I triumphed, and I now go abroad, leaving Frank and his Mary made happy by the possession of what could only have been a burden to me.

So the MS ends. Major Thunder fell in battle a few years after the adventure it relates. Frank O'Brien's grandchildren hear of him with gratitude and awe. The Rath has been long since totally dismantled and left to go to ruin.

GEORGE MOORE

A Play-House in the Waste

'It's a closed mouth that can hold a good story,' as the saying goes, and very soon it got about that Father MacTurnan had written to Rome saying he was willing to take a wife to his bosom for patriotic reasons, if the Pope would relieve him of his vow of celibacy. And many phrases and words from his letter (translated by whom—by the Bishop or Father Meehan? Nobody ever knew) were related over the Dublin firesides, till at last out of the talk a tall gaunt man emerged, in an old overcoat green from weather and wear, the tails of it flapping as he rode his bicycle through the great waste bog that lies between Belmullet and Crossmolina. His name! We liked it. It appealed to our imagination. MacTurnan! It conveyed something from afar like Hamlet or Don Quixote. He seemed as near and as far from us as they, till Pat Comer, one of the organizers of the IAOS, came in and said, after listening to the talk that was going round:

'Is it of the priest that rides in the great Mayo bog you are speaking? If it is, you haven't got the story rightly.' As he told us the story, so it is printed in this book. And we sat wondering greatly, for we seemed to see a soul on its way to heaven. But round a fire there is always one who cannot get off the subject of women and blasphemy—a papist generally he is; and it was Quinn that evening who kept plaguing us with jokes, whether it would be a fat girl or a thin that the priest would choose if the Pope gave him leave to marry, until at last, losing all patience with him, I bade him be silent, and asked Pat Comer to tell us if the priest was meditating a new plan for Ireland's salvation.

'For a mind like his,' I said, 'would not stand still and problems such as ours waiting to be solved.'

'You're wrong there! He thinks no more of Ireland, and neither reads nor plans, but knits stockings ever since the wind took his play-house away.'

'Took his play-house away!' said several.

'And why would he be building a play-house,' somebody asked, 'and he living in a waste?'

'A queer idea, surely!' said another. 'A play-house in the waste!'

'Yes, a queer idea,' said Pat, 'but a true one all the same, for I have seen it with my own eyes—or the ruins of it, and not later back than three weeks ago, when I was staying with the priest himself. You know the road, all of you—how it straggles from Foxford through the bog alongside of bog-holes deep enough to drown one, and into which the jarvey and myself seemed in great likelihood of pitching, for the car went down into great ruts, and the horse was shying from one side of the road to the other, and at nothing so far as we could see.'

'There's nothing to be afeared of, yer honour; only once was he near leaving the road, the day before Christmas, and I driving the doctor. It was here he saw it—a white thing gliding, and the wheel of the car must have gone within an inch of the bog-hole.'

'And the doctor. Did he see it?' I said.

'He saw it too, and so scared was he that the hair rose up and went through his cap.'

'Did the jarvey laugh when he said that?' we asked Pat Comer; and Pat answered: 'Not he! Them fellows just speak as the words come to them without thinking. Let me get on with my story. We drove on for about a mile, and it was to stop him from clicking his tongue at the horse that I asked him if the bog was Father MacTurnan's parish.'

'Every mile of it, sir,' he said, 'every mile of it, and we do be seeing him buttoned up in his old coat riding along the roads on his bicycle going to sick calls.'

'Do you often be coming this road?' says I.

'Not very often, sir. No one lives here except the poor people, and the priest and the doctor. Faith! there isn't a poorer parish in Ireland, and every one of them would have been dead long ago if it had not been for Father James.'

'And how does he help them?'

'Isn't he always writing letters to the Government asking for relief works? Do you see those bits of roads?'

'Where do those roads lead to?'

'Nowhere. Them roads stops in the middle of the bog when the money is out.'

'But,' I said, 'surely it would be better if the money were spent upon permanent improvements—on drainage, for instance.'

The jarvey didn't answer; he called to his horse, and not being able to stand the clicking of his tongue, I kept on about the drainage.

'There's no fall, sir.'

'And the bog is too big,' I added, in hope of encouraging conversation.

'Faith it is, sir.'

'But we aren't very far from the sea, are we?'

'About a couple of miles.'

'Well then,' I said, 'couldn't a harbour be made?'

'They were thinking about that, but there's no depth of water, and everyone's against emigration now.'

'Ah! the harbour would encourage emigration.'

'So it would, your honour.'

'But is there no talk about home industries, weaving, lace-making?'

'I won't say that.'

'But has it been tried?'

'The candle do be burning in the priest's window till one in the morning, and he sitting up thinking of plans to keep the people at home. Now, do ye see that house, sir, fornint my whip at the top of the hill? Well, that's the play-house he built.'

'A play-house?'

'Yes, yer honour. Father James hoped the people might come

from Dublin to see it, for no play like it had ever been acted in Ireland before, sir!'

'And was the play performed?'

'No, yer honour. The priest had been learning them all the summer, but the autumn was on them before they had got it by rote, and a wind came and blew down one of the walls.'

'And couldn't Father MacTurnan get the money to build it up?'

'Sure, he might have got the money, but where'd be the use when there was no luck in it?'

'And who were to act the play?'

'The girls and the boys in the parish, and the prettiest girl in all the parish was to play Good Deeds.'

'So it was a miracle play,' I said.

'Do you see that man? It's the priest coming out of Tom Burke's cabin, and I warrant he do be bringing him the Sacrament, and he having the holy oils with him, for Tom won't pass the day; we had the worst news of him last night.'

'And I can tell you,' said Pat Comer, dropping his story for a moment and looking round the circle, 'it was a sad story the jarvey told me. He told it well, for I can see the one-roomed hovel full of peat-smoke, the black iron pot with traces of the yellow stirabout in it on the hearth, and the sick man on the pallet bed, and the priest by his side mumbling prayers together. Faith! these jarveys can tell a story—none better.'

'As well as yourself, Pat,' one of us said. And Pat began to tell of the miles of bog on either side of the straggling road, of the hilltop to the left, with the play-house showing against the dark and changing clouds; of a woman in a red petticoat, a handkerchief tied round her head, who had flung down her spade the moment she caught sight of the car, of the man who appeared on the brow and blew a horn. 'For she mistook us for bailiffs,' said Pat, 'and two little sheep hardly bigger than geese were driven away.'

'A play-house in the waste for these people,' I was saying to myself all the time, till my meditations were interrupted by the jarvey telling that the rocky river we crossed was called the Greyhound—a not inappropriate name, for it ran swiftly. . . . Away

down the long road a white cottage appeared, and the jarvey said
to me, 'That is the priest's house.' It stood on the hillside some
little way from the road, and all the way to the door I wondered
how his days passed in the great loneliness of the bog.

'His reverence isn't at home, yer honour—he's gone to attend a
sick call.'

'Yes, I know—Tom Burke.'

'And is Tom better, Mike?'

'The devil a bether he'll be this side of Jordan,' the jarvey
answered, and the housekeeper showed me into the priest's parlour. It was lined with books, and I looked forward to a pleasant
chat when we had finished our business. At that time I was on a
relief committee, and the people were starving in the poor parts of
the country.

'I think he'll be back in about an hour's time, yer honour.' But
the priest seemed to be detained longer than his housekeeper
expected, and the moaning of the wind round the cottage
reminded me of the small white thing the horse and the doctor had
seen gliding along the road. 'The priest knows the story—he will
tell me,' I said, and piled more turf on the fire—fine sods of hard
black turf they were, and well do I remember seeing them melting
away. But all of a sudden my eyes closed. I couldn't have been asleep
more than a few minutes when it seemed to me a great crowd of
men and women had gathered about the house, and a moment
after the door was flung open, and a tall, gaunt man faced me.

'I've just come,' he said, 'from a deathbed, and they that have followed me aren't far from death if we don't succeed in getting help.'

I don't know how I can tell you of the crowd I saw round the
house that day. We are accustomed to see poor people in towns
cowering under arches, but it is more pitiful to see people starving
in the fields on the mountainside. I don't know why it should be so,
but it is. But I call to mind two men in ragged trousers and shirts as
ragged, with brown beards on faces yellow with famine; and the
words of one of them are not easily forgotten: 'The white sun of
Heaven doesn't shine upon two poorer men than upon this man
and myself.' I can tell you I didn't envy the priest his job, living all

his life in the waste listening to tales of starvation, looking into famished faces. There were some women among them, kept back by the men, who wanted to get their word in first. They seemed to like to talk about their misery . . . and I said:

'They are tired of seeing each other. I am a spectacle, a show, an amusement for them. I don't know if you can catch my meaning?'

'I think I do,' Father James answered. And I asked him to come for a walk up the hill and show me the play-house.

Again he hesitated, and I said: 'You must come, Father MacTurnan, for a walk. You must forget the misfortunes of those people for a while.' He yielded, and we spoke of the excellence of the road under our feet, and he told me that when he conceived the idea of a play-house, he had already succeeded in persuading the inspector to agree that the road they were making should go to the top of the hill. 'The policy of the Government,' he said, 'from the first was that relief works should benefit nobody except the workers, and it is sometimes very difficult to think out a project for work that will be perfectly useless. Arches have been built on the top of hills, and roads that lead nowhere. A strange sight to the stranger a road must be that stops suddenly in the middle of a bog. One wonders at first how a Government could be so foolish, but when one thinks of it, it is easy to understand that the Government doesn't wish to spend money on works that will benefit a class. But the road that leads nowhere is difficult to make, even though starving men are employed upon it; for a man to work well there must be an end in view, and I can tell you it is difficult to bring even starving men to engage on a road that leads nowhere. If I'd told everything I am telling you to the inspector, he wouldn't have agreed to let the road run to the top of the hill; but I said to him: "The road leads nowhere; as well let it end at the top of the hill as down in the valley." So I got the money for my road and some money for my play-house, for of course the play-house was as useless as the road; a play-house in the waste can neither interest or benefit anybody! But there was an idea at the back of my mind all the time that when the road and the play-house were finished, I might be able to induce the Government to build a harbour.'

'But the harbour would be of use.'

'Of very little,' he answered. 'For the harbour to be of use a great deal of dredging would have to be done.'

'And the Government needn't undertake the dredging. How very ingenious! I suppose you often come here to read your breviary?'

'During the building of the play-house I often used to be up here, and during the rehearsals I was here every day.'

'If there was a rehearsal,' I said to myself, 'there must have been a play.' And I affected interest in the grey shallow sea and the erosion of the low-lying land—a salt marsh filled with pools.

'I thought once,' said the priest, 'that if the play were a great success, a line of flat-bottomed steamers might be built.'

'Sitting here in the quiet evenings,' I said to myself, 'reading his breviary, dreaming of a line of steamships crowded with visitors! He has been reading about the Oberammergau performances.' So that was his game—the road, the play-house, the harbour—and I agreed with him that no one would have dared to predict that visitors would have come from all sides of Europe to see a few peasants performing a   miracle play in the Tyrol.

'Come,' I said, 'into the play-house and let me see how you built it.'

Half a wall and some of the roof had fallen, and the rubble had not been cleared away, and I said:

'It will cost many pounds to repair the damage, but having gone so far you should give the play a chance.'

'I don't think it would be advisable,' he muttered, half to himself, half to me.

As you may well imagine, I was anxious to hear if he had discovered any aptitude for acting among the girls and the boys who lived in the cabins.

'I think,' he answered me, 'that the play would have been fairly acted; I think that, with a little practice, we might have done as well as they did at Oberammergau.'

An odd man, more willing to discuss the play that he had chosen than the talents of those who were going to perform it, and he told me that it had been written in the fourteenth century in Latin, and that he had translated it into Irish.

I asked him if it would have been possible to organize an excursion from Dublin—'Oberammergau in the West.'

'I used to think so. But it is eight miles from Rathowen, and the road is a bad one, and when they got here there would be no place for them to stay; they would have to go all the way back again, and that would be sixteen miles.

'Yet you did well, Father James, to build the play-house, for the people could work better while they thought they were accomplishing something. Let me start a subscription for you in Dublin.'

'I don't think that it would be possible——'

'Not for me to get fifty pounds?'

'You might get the money, but I don't think we could ever get a performance of the play.'

'And why not?' I said.

'You see, the wind came and blew down the wall. The people are very pious; I think they felt that the time they spent rehearsing might have been better spent. The play-house disturbed them in their ideas. They hear Mass on Sundays, and there are the Sacraments, and they remember they have to die. It used to seem to me a very sad thing to see all the people going to America; the poor Celt disappearing in America, leaving his own country, leaving his language, and very often his religion.'

'And does it no longer seem to you sad that such a thing should happen?'

'No, not if it is the will of God. God has specially chosen the Irish race to convert the world. No race has provided so many missionaries, no race has preached the Gospel more frequently to the heathen; and once we realize that we have to die, and very soon, and that the Catholic Church is the only true Church, our ideas about race and nationality fade from us. *We* are here, not to make life successful and triumphant, but to gain heaven. That is the truth, and it is to the honour of the Irish people that they have been selected by God to preach the truth, even though they lose their nationality in preaching it. I do not expect you to accept these opinions. I know that you think very differently, but living here I have learned to acquiesce in the will of God.'

He stopped speaking suddenly, like one ashamed of having expressed himself too openly, and soon after we were met by a number of peasants, and the priest's attention was engaged; the inspector of the relief works had to speak to him; and I didn't see him again until dinner-time.

'You have given them hope,' he said.

This was gratifying to hear, and the priest sat listening while I told him of the looms already established in different parts of the country. We talked about half an hour, and then like one who suddenly remembers, the priest got up and fetched his knitting.

'Do you knit every evening?'

'I have got into the way of knitting lately—it passes the time.'

'But do you never read?' I asked, and my eyes went towards the bookshelves.

'I used to read a great deal. But there wasn't a woman in the parish that could turn a heel properly, so I had to learn to knit.'

'Do you like knitting better than reading?' I asked, feeling ashamed of my curiosity.

'I have constantly to attend sick calls, and if one is absorbed in a book one doesn't like to put it aside.'

'I see you have two volumes of miracle plays!'

'Yes, and that's another danger: a book begets all kinds of ideas and notions into one's head. The idea of that play-house came out of those books.'

'But,' I said, 'you don't think that God sent the storm because He didn't wish a play to be performed?'

'One cannot judge God's designs. Whether God sent the storm or whether it was accident must remain a matter for conjecture; but it is not a matter of conjecture that one is doing certain good by devoting oneself to one's daily task, getting the Government to start new relief works, establishing schools for weaving. The people are entirely dependent upon me, and when I'm attending to their wants I know I'm doing right.'

The play-house interested me more than the priest's ideas of

right and wrong, and I tried to get him back to it; but the subject
seemed a painful one, and I said to myself: 'The jarvey will tell me
all about it tomorrow. I can rely on him to find out the whole story
from the housekeeper in the kitchen.' And sure enough, we hadn't
got to the Greyhound River before he was leaning across the well
of the car talking to me and asking if the priest was thinking of
putting up the wall of the play-house.

'The wall of the play-house?' I said.

'Yes, yer honour. Didn't I see both of you going up the hill in the
evening time?'

'I don't think we shall ever see a play in the play-house.'

'Why would we, since it was God that sent the wind that blew it
down?'

'How do you know it was God that sent the wind? It might have
been the devil himself, or somebody's curse.'

'Sure it is of Mrs Sheridan you do be thinking, yer honour, and
of her daughter—she that was to be playing Good Deeds in the
play, yer honour; and wasn't she wake coming home from the
learning of the play? And when the signs of her wakeness began to
show, the widow Sheridan took a halter off the cow and tied Margaret to the wall, and she was in the stable till the child was born.
Then didn't her mother take a bit of string and tie it round the
child's throat, and bury it near the play-house; and it was three
nights after that the storm rose, and the child pulled the thatch out
of the roof.'

'But did she murder the child?'

'Sorra wan of me knows. She sent for the priest when she was
dying, and told him what she had done.'

'But the priest wouldn't tell what he heard in the confessional,' I
said.

'Mrs Sheridan didn't die that night; not till the end of the week,
and the neighbours heard her talking of the child she had buried,
and then they all knew what the white thing was they had seen by
the roadside. The night the priest left her he saw the white thing
standing in front of him, and if he hadn't been a priest he'd have
dropped down dead; so he took some water from the bog-hole and

dashed it over it, saying, "I baptize thee in the name of the Father, and of the Son, and of the Holy Ghost!" '

The driver told his story like one saying his prayers, and he seemed to have forgotten that he had a listener.

'It must have been a great shock to the priest.'

'Faith it was, sir, to meet an unbaptized child on the roadside, and that child the only bastard that was ever born in the parish—so Tom Mulhare says, and he's the oldest man in the county.'

'It was altogether a very queer idea—this play-house.'

'It was indeed, sir, a quare idea, but you see he's a quare man. He has been always thinking of something to do good, and it is said that he thinks too much. Father James is a very quare man, your honour.'

6

FORREST REID

Courage

When the children came to stay with their grandfather, young Michael Aherne, walking with the others from the station to the rectory, noticed the high grey wall that lined one side of the long, sleepy lane, and wondered what lay beyond it. Far above his head, over the tops of the mossy stones, trees stretched green arms that beckoned to him, and threw black shadows on the white, dusty road. His four brothers and sisters, stepping demurely beside tall, rustling Aunt Caroline, left him lagging behind, and, when a white bird fluttered out for a moment into the sunlight, they did not even see it. Michael called to them, and eight eyes turned straightaway to the trees, but were too late. So he trotted on and took fat, tired Barbara's place by Aunt Caroline.

'Does anybody live there?' he asked; but Aunt Caroline shook her head. The house, whose chimneys he presently caught a glimpse of through the trees, had been empty for years and years; the people to whom it belonged lived somewhere else.

Michael learned more than this from Rebecca, the cook, who told him that the house was empty because it was haunted. Long ago a lady lived there, but she had been very wicked and very unhappy, poor thing, and even now could find no rest in her grave. . . .

It was on an afternoon when he was all alone that Michael set out to explore the stream running past the foot of the rectory garden. He would follow it, he thought, wherever it led him; follow it just as his father, far away in wild places, had followed mighty rivers into the heart of the forest. The long, sweet, green grass brushed against his legs, and a white cow, with a buttercup hanging from the corner of her mouth, gazed at him in mild amazement as he flew past. He kept to the meadow side, and on the opposite bank the leaning trees made little magic caves tapestried with green. Black flies darted restlessly about, and every now and again he heard strange splashes—splashes of birds, of fish; the splash of a rat; and once the heavy, floundering splash of the cow herself, plunging into the water up to her knees. He watched her tramp through the sword-shaped leaves of a bed of irises, while the rich black mud oozed up between patches of bright green weed. A score of birds made a quaint chorus of trills and peeps, chuckles and whistles; a wren, like a tiny winged mouse, flitted about the ivy-covered bole of a hollow elm. Then Michael came unexpectedly to the end of his journey, for an iron gate was swung here right across the stream, and on either side of it, as far as he could see, stretched a high grey wall.

He paused. The gate was padlocked, and its spiked bars were so narrow that to climb it would not be easy. Suddenly a white bird rose out of the burning green and gold of the trees, and for a moment, in the sunlight, it was the whitest thing in the world. Then it flew back again into the mysterious shadow, and Michael stood breathless.

He knew now where he was, knew that this wall must be a continuation of the wall in the lane. The stooping trees leaned down as if to catch him in their arms. He looked at the padlock on the gate and saw that it was half eaten by rust. He took off his shoes and stockings. Stringing them about his neck, he waded through the water and with a stone struck the padlock once, twice—twice only, for at the second blow the lock dropped into the stream, with a dull splash. Michael tugged at the rusty bolt, and in a moment or two the gate was open. On the other side he clambered up the bank to put on his shoes, and it was then that, as he glanced behind him, he saw the gate swing slowly back in silence.

That was all, yet it somehow startled him, and he had a fantastic impression that he had not been meant to see it. 'Of course it must have moved of its own weight,' he told himself, but it gave him an uneasy feeling as of some one following stealthily on his footsteps, and he remembered Rebecca's story.

Before him was a dark, moss-grown path, like the narrow aisle of a huge cathedral whose pillars were the over-arching trees. It seemed to lead on and on through an endless green stillness, and he stood dreaming on the outermost fringe, wondering, doubting, not very eager to explore further.

He walked on, and the noise of the stream died away behind him, like the last warning murmur of the friendly world outside. Suddenly, turning at an abrupt angle, he came upon the house. It lay beyond what had once been a lawn, and the grass, coarse and matted, grew right up to the doorsteps, which were green, with gaping apertures between the stones. Ugly, livid stains, lines of dark moss and lichen, crept over the red bricks; and the shutters and blinds looked as if they had been closed for ever. Then Michael's heart gave a jump, for at that moment an uneasy puff of wind stirred one of the lower shutters, which flapped back with a dismal rattle.

He stood there while he might have counted a hundred, on the verge of flight, poised between curiosity and fear. At length curiosity, the spirit of adventure, triumphed, and he advanced to a closer inspection. With his nose pressed to the pane, he gazed into a large dark room, across which lay a band of sunlight, thin as a stretched ribbon. He gave the window a tentative push, and, to his surprise, it yielded. Had there been another visitor here? he wondered. For he saw that the latch was not broken, must have been drawn back from within, or forced, very skilfully, in some way that had left no mark upon the woodwork. He made these reflections and then, screwing up his courage, stepped across the sill.

Once inside, he had a curious sense of relief. He could somehow *feel* that the house was empty, that not even the ghost of a ghost lingered there. With this certainty, everything dropped consolingly, yet half disappointingly, back into the commonplace, and he became conscious that outside it was broad daylight, and that ghost stories were nothing more than a kind of fairy-tale. He opened the other shutters, letting the rich afternoon light pour in. Though the house had been empty for so long, it smelt sweet and fresh, and not a speck of dust was visible anywhere. He drew his fingers over the top of one of the little tables, but so clean was it that it might have been polished that morning. He touched the faded silks and curtains, and sniffed at faintly smelling china jars. Over the wide carved chimney-piece hung a picture of a lady, very young and beautiful. She was sitting in a chair, and beside her stood a tall, delicate boy of Michael's own age. One of the boy's hands rested on the lady's shoulder, and the other held a gilt-clasped book. Michael, gazing at them, easily saw that they were mother and son. The lady seemed to him infinitely lovely, and presently she made him think of his own mother, and with that he began to feel homesick, and all kinds of memories returned to him. They were dim and shadowy, and, as he stood there dreaming, it seemed to him that somehow his mother was bound up with this other lady—he could not tell how—and at last he turned away, wishing that he had not looked at the picture. He drew from his pocket the letter he had received that morning. His mother was better; she would soon be quite well again. Yesterday she had been out driving for more than an hour, she told him, and today she felt a little tired, which was why her letter must be rather short. . . . And he remembered, remembered through a sense of menacing trouble only half realized during those days of uneasy waiting in the silent rooms at home; only half realized even at the actual moment of goodbye—remembered that last glimpse of her face, smiling, smiling so beautifully and bravely. . . .

He went out into the hall and unbarred and flung wide the front door, before ascending to the upper storeys. He found many curious things, but, above all, in one large room, he discovered a whole store of toys—soldiers, puzzles, books, a bow and arrows, a musical box with a little silver key lying beside it. He wound it up, and a gay, sweet melody tinkled out into the silence, thin and fragile, losing itself in the empty vastness of that still house, like the flicker of a taper in a cave.

He opened a door leading into a second room, a bedroom, and, sitting down in the window-seat, began to turn the pages of an old illuminated volume he found there, full of strange pictures of saints and martyrs, all glowing in gold and bright colours, yet somehow sinister, disquieting. It was with a start that, as he looked up, he noticed how dark it had become indoors. The pattern had faded out of the chintz bed curtains, and he could no longer see clearly into the further corners of the room. It was from these corners that the darkness seemed to be stealing out, like a thin smoke, spreading slowly over everything. Then a strange fancy came to him, and it seemed to him that he had lived in this house for years and years, and that all his other life was but a dream. It was so dark now that the bed curtains were like pale shadows, and outside, over the trees, the moon was growing brighter. He must go home. . . .

He sat motionless, trying to realize what had happened, listening, listening, for it was as if the secret, hidden heart of the house had begun very faintly to beat. Faintly at first, a mere stirring of the vacant atmosphere, yet, as the minutes passed, it gathered strength, and with this consciousness of awakening life a fear came also. He listened in the darkness, and though he could hear nothing, he had a vivid sense that he was no longer alone. Whatever had dwelt here before had come back, was perhaps even now creeping up the stairs. A sickening, stupefying dread paralysed him. It had not come for him, he told himself—whatever it was. It wanted to avoid him, and perhaps he could get downstairs without meeting it. Then it flashed across his mind, radiantly, savingly, that if he had not seen it by now it was only because it *was* avoiding him. He sprang to his feet and opened the door—not the door leading to the other room, but one giving on the landing.

Outside, the great well of the staircase was like a yawning pit of blackness. His heart thumped as he stood clutching at the wall. With shut eyes, lest he should see something he had no desire to see, he took two steps forward and gripped the balusters. Then, with eyes still tightly shut, he ran quickly down—quickly, recklessly, as if a fire were at his heels.

Down in the hall, the open door showed as a dim silver-grey square, and he ran to it, but the instant he passed the threshold his panic left him. A fear remained, but it was no longer blind and brutal. It was as if a voice had spoken to him, and, as he stood there, a sense that everything swayed in a balance, that everything depended upon what he did next, swept over him. He looked up at the dark, dreadful staircase. Nothing had pursued him, and he knew now that nothing *would* pursue him. Whatever was there was not there for that purpose, and if he were to see it he must go in search of it. But if he left it? If he left it now, he knew that he should leave something else as well. In forsaking one he should forsake both; in losing one he should lose both. Another spirit at this moment was close to him, and it was the spirit of his mother, who, invisible, seemed to hold his hand and keep him there upon the step. But why—why? He could only tell that she *wanted* him to stay: but of that he was certain. If he were a coward she would know. It would be impossible to hide it from her. She might forgive him—she would forgive him—but it could never be the same again. He steadied himself against the side of the porch. The cold moonlight washed through the dim hall, and turned to a glimmering greyness the lowest flight of stairs. With sobbing breath and wide eyes he retraced his steps, but at the foot of the stairs he stopped once more. The greyness ended at the first landing; beyond that, an impenetrable blackness led to those awful upper storeys. He put his foot on the lowest stair, and slowly, step by step, he mounted, clutching the balusters. He did not pause on the landing, but walked on into the darkness, which seemed to close about his slight figure like the heavy wings of a monstrous tomb.

On the uppermost landing of all, the open doors allowed a faint light to penetrate. He entered the room of the toys and stood beside the table. The beating of the blood in his ears almost deafened him. 'If only it would come now!' he prayed, for he felt that he could not tolerate the strain of waiting. But nothing came; there was neither sight nor sound. At length he made his final effort, and crossing to the door, which was now closed, turned the handle. For a moment the room seemed empty, and he was conscious of a sudden, an immense relief. Then, close by the window-seat, in the dim twilight, he perceived something. He stood still, while a deathly coldness descended upon him. At first hardly more than a shadow, a thickening of the darkness, what he gazed upon made no movement, and so long as it remained thus, with head mercifully lowered, he felt that he could bear it. But the suspense tortured him, and presently a faint moan of anguish rose from his dry lips. With that, the grey, marred face, the face he dreaded to see, was slowly lifted. He tried to close his eyes, but could not. He felt himself sinking to the ground, and clutched at the doorpost for support. Then suddenly he seemed to know that it, too, this—this thing—was afraid, and that what it feared was his fear. He saw the torment, the doubt and despair, that glowed in the smoky dimness of those hollowed, dreadful eyes. How changed was this lady from the bright, beautiful lady of the picture! He felt a pity for her, and as his compassion grew his fear diminished. He watched her move slowly towards him—nearer, nearer—only now there was something else that mingled with his dread, battling with it, overcoming it; and when at last she held out her arms to him, held them wide in a supreme, soundless appeal, he knew that it had conquered. He came forward and lifted his face to hers. At the same instant she bent down over him and seemed to draw him to her. An icy coldness, as of a dense mist, enfolded him, and he felt and saw no more. . . .

When he opened his eyes the moon was shining upon him, and he knew at once that he was alone. He knew, moreover, that he was now free to go. But the house no longer held any terror for him, and, as he scrambled to his feet, he felt a strange happiness that was very quiet, and a little like that he used to feel when, after he had gone up to bed, he lay growing sleepier and sleepier, while he listened to his mother singing. He must go home, but he would not go for a minute or two yet. He moved his hand, and it struck against a box of matches lying on a table. He had not known they were there, but now he lighted the tall candles on the chimneypiece, and as he did so he became more vividly aware of what he had felt dimly ever since he had opened his eyes. Some subtle atmospheric change had come about, though in what it consisted he could not at once tell. It was like a hush in the air, the strange hush which comes with the falling of snow. But how could there be snow in August? and, moreover, this was within the house, not outside. He lifted one of the candlesticks and saw that a delicate powder of dust had gathered upon it. He looked down at his own clothes—they, too, were covered with that same thin powder. Then he knew what was happening. The dust of years had begun to fall again; silently, slowly, like a soft and continuous caress, laying everything in the house to sleep.

Dawn was breaking when, with a candle in either hand, he descended the broad, whitening staircase. As he passed out into the garden he saw lanterns approaching, and knew they had come to look for him. They were very kind, very gentle with him, and it was not till the next day that he learned of the telegram which had come in his absence.

7

DOROTHY MACARDLE

The Prisoner

It was on an evening late in May that Liam Daly startled us by strolling into Una's room, a thin, laughing shadow of the boy we had known at home. We had imagined him a helpless convalescent still in Ireland and welcomed him as if he had risen from the dead. For a while there was nothing but clamourous question and answer, raillery, revelry and the telling of news; his thirty-eight days' hunger-strike had already become a theme of whimsical wit; but once or twice as he talked his face sobered and he hesitated, gazing at me with a pondering, burdened look.

'He holds me with his glittering eye!' I complained at last. He laughed.

'Actually,' he said, 'you're right. There *is* a story I have to tell—sometime, somewhere, and if you'll listen, I couldn't do better than to tell it here and now.'

He had found an eager audience, but his grave face quieted us and it was in an intent silence that he told his inexplicable tale.

'You'll say it was a dream,' he began, 'and I hope you'll be right; I could never make up my mind; it happened in the gaol. You know Kilmainham?' He smiled at Larry who nodded. 'The gloomiest prison in Ireland, I suppose—goodness knows how old. When the strike started I was in a punishment cell, a "noisome dungeon", right enough, complete with rats and all, dark always, and dead quiet; none of the others were in that wing. It amounted to solitary confinement, of course, and on hunger-strike that's bad, the trouble is to keep a hold of your mind.

'I think it was about the thirtieth day I began to be afraid—afraid of going queer. It's not a pretty story, all this,' he broke off, looking remorsefully at Una, 'but I'd like you to understand—I want to know what you think.

'They'd given up bringing in food and the doctor didn't trouble himself overmuch with me; sometimes a warder would look through the peep-hole and shout a remark; but most of the day and all night I was alone.

'The worst was losing the sense of time; you've no idea how that torments you. I'd doze and wake up and not know whether a day or only an hour had gone; I'd think sometimes it was the fiftieth day, maybe, and we'd surely be out soon; then I'd think it was the thirtieth still; then a crazy notion would come that there was no such thing as time in prison at all; I don't know how to explain—I used to think that time went past outside like a stream, moving on, but in prison you were in a kind of whirlpool—time going round and round with you, so that you'd never come to anything, even death, only back again to yesterday and round to today and back to yesterday again. I got terrified, then, of going mad; I began talking and chattering to myself, trying to keep myself company, and that only made me worse because I found I couldn't stop—something seemed to have got into my brain and to be talking—talking hideous, blasphemous things, and I couldn't stop it. I thought I was turning into that—Ah, there's no describing it!

'At times I'd fight my way out of it and pray. I knew, at those times, that the blaspheming thing wasn't myself; I thought 'twas a foul spirit, some old criminal maybe, that had died in that cell. Then the fear would come on me that if I died insane he'd take possession of me and I'd get lost in Hell. I gave up praying for everything except the one thing, then—that I'd die before I went mad. One living soul to talk to would have saved me; when the doctor came I'd all I could do to keep from crying out to him not to leave me alone; but I'd just sense enough left to hold on while he was there.

'The solitude and the darkness were like one—the one enemy—you couldn't hear and you couldn't see. At times it was pitch black;

77

I'd think I was in my coffin then and the silence trying to smother me. Then I'd seem to float up and away—to lose my body, and then wake up suddenly in a cold sweat, my heart drumming with the shock. The darkness and I were two things hating one another, striving to destroy one another—it closing on me, crushing me, stifling the life out of my brain—I trying to pierce it, trying to see— My God, it was awful!

'One black night the climax came. I thought I was dying and that 'twas a race between madness and death. I was striving to keep my mind clear till my heart would stop, praying to go sane to God. And the darkness was against me—the darkness, thick and power-ful and black. I said to myself that if I could pierce that, if I could make myself see—see anything, I'd not go mad. I put out all the strength I had, striving to see the window or the peep-hole or the crucifix on the wall, and failed. I knew there was a little iron seat clamped into the wall in the corner opposite the bed. I willed, with a desperate, frenzied intensity, to see that; and I did see it at last. And when I saw it all the fear and strain died away in me, because I saw that I was not alone.

'He was sitting there quite still, a limp, despairing figure, his head bowed, his hands hanging between his knees; for a long time I waited, then I was able to see better and I saw that he was a boy— fair-haired, white-faced, quite young, and there were fetters on his feet. I can tell you, my heart went out to him, in pity and thankful-ness and love.

'After a while he moved, lifted up his head and stared at me—the most piteous look I have ever seen.

'He was a young lad with thin, starved features and deep eye-sockets like a skull's; he looked, then bowed his head down hope-lessly again, not saying a word. But I knew that his whole torment was the need to speak, to tell something; I got quite strong and calm, watching him, waiting for him to speak.

'I waited a long while, and that dizzy sense of time working in a circle took me, the circles getting larger and larger, like eddies in a pool, again. At last he looked up and rested his eyes beseechingly on me as if imploring me to be patient; I understood; I had conquered the dark—he had to break through the silence—I knew it was very hard.

'I saw his lips move and at last I heard him—a thin, weak whisper came to me: "Listen—listen—for the love of God!"

'I looked at him, waiting; I didn't speak; it would have scared him. He leaned forward, swaying, his eyes fixed, not on mine, but on some awful vision of their own; the eyes of a soul in purgatory, glazed with pain.

' "Listen, listen!" I heard, "the truth! You must tell it—it must be remembered; it must be written down!"

' "I will tell it," I said, very gently, "I will tell it if I live."

' "Live, live, and tell it!" he said, moaningly and then, then he began. I can't repeat his words, all broken, shuddering phrases; he talked as if to himself only—I'll remember as best I can.

' "My mother, my mother!" he kept moaning, and "the name of shame!" "They'll put the name of shame on us," he said, "and my mother that is so proud—so proud she never let a tear fall, though they murdered my father before her eyes! Listen to me!" He seemed in an anguish of haste and fear, striving to tell me before we'd be lost again. "Listen! Would I do it to save my life? God knows I wouldn't, and I won't! But they'll say I did it! They'll say it to her. They'll be pouring out their lies through Ireland and I cold in my grave!"

'His thin body was shaken with anguish; I didn't know what to do for him. At last I said, "Sure, no one'll believe their lies."

' "My Lord won't believe it!" he said vehemently. "Didn't he send me up and down with messages to his lady? Would he do that if he didn't know I loved him—know I could go to any death?"

' " 'Twas in the Duke's Lawn they caught me," he went on. " 'Twas on Sunday last and they're starving me ever since; trying night and day they are to make me tell them what house he's in—and God knows I could tell them! I could tell!"

'I knew well the dread that was on him. I said, "There's no fear," and he looked at me a little quieter then.

' "They beat me," he went on. "They half strangled me in the Castle Yard and then they threw me in here. Listen to me! Are you listening?" he kept imploring. "I'll not have time to tell you all!"

' "Yesterday one of the redcoats came to me—an officer, I suppose, and he told me my Lord will be caught. Some lad that took
his last message sold him. . . . He's going to Moira House in the
morning, disguised; they'll waylay him—attack him in the street.
They say there'll be a fight—and sure I know there will—and he'll
be alone; they'll kill him. He laughed, the devil—telling me that!
He laughed, I tell you, because I cried.

' "A priest came in to me then—a priest! My God, he was a fiend!
He came in to me in the dead of night, when I was lying shivering
and sobbing for my Lord. He sat and talked to me in a soft voice—
I thought at first he was kind. Listen till I tell you! Listen till you
hear all! He told me I could save my Lord's life. They'd go quietly
to his house and take him; there'd be no fighting and he'd not be
hurt. I'd only have to say where his lodging was. My God, I stood
up and cursed him! He, a priest! God forgive me if he was."

' "He was no priest," I said, trying to quiet him. "That's an old
tale."

' "He went out then," the poor boy went on, talking feverishly,
against time. "And a man I'd seen at the Castle came in, a man with
a narrow face and a black cloak. The priest was with him and he
began talking to me again, the other listening, but I didn't mind
him or answer him at all. He asked me wasn't my mother a poor
widow, and wasn't I her only son. Wouldn't I do well to take her to
America, he said, out of the hurt and harm, and make a warm
home for her, where she could end her days in peace. I could earn
the right to it, he said—good money, and the passage out, and
wasn't it my duty as a son. The face of my mother came before
me—the proud, sweet look she has, like a queen; I minded the lov-
ing voice of her and she saying, 'I gave your father for Ireland and
I'd give you.' My God, my God, what were they but fiends? What
will I do, what will I do at all?"

'He was in an agony, twisting his thin hands.

' "You'll die and leave her her pride in you," I said.

'Then, in broken gasps he told me the rest.

' "The Castle man—he was tall, he stood over me—he said,
'You'll tell us what we want to know.'"

' "I'll die first," I said to him and he smiled. He had thin, twisted lips—and he said, "You'll hang in the morning like a dog."

' "Like an Irishman, please God," I said.

' "He went mad at that and shook his fist in my face and talked sharp and wicked through his teeth. O my God! I went down on my knees to him, I asked him in God's holy name! How will I bear it? How will I bear it at all?"

'He was overwhelmed with woe and terror; he bowed his head and trembled from head to foot.

' "They'll hang me in the morning," he gasped, looking at me haggardly. "And they'll take him and they'll tell him I informed. The black priest'll go to my mother—he said it! Himself said it! He'll tell her I informed! It will be the death blow on her heart—worse than death! 'Twill be written in the books of Ireland to the end of time. They'll cast the word of shame on my grave."

'I never saw a creature in such pain—it would break your heart. I put out all the strength I had and swore an oath to him. I swore that if I lived I'd give out the truth, get it told and written through Ireland. I don't know if he heard; he looked at me wearily, exhausted, and sighed and leaned his head back against the wall.

'I was tired out and half conscious only, but there was a thing I was wanting to ask. For a while I couldn't remember what it was, then I remembered again and asked it: "Tell me, what is your name?"

'I could hardly see him. The darkness had taken him again, and the silence; his voice was very far off and faint.

' "I forget," it said. "I have forgotten. I can't remember my name."

'It was quite dark then. I believe I fainted. I was unconscious when I was released.'

Max Barry broke the puzzled silence with a wondering exclamation: 'Lord Edward! More than a hundred years!'

'Poor wretch!' laughed the irrepressible Frank. 'In Kilmainham since ninety-eight!'

'Ninety-eight?' Larry looked up quickly. 'You weren't in the hospital were you, Liam? I was. You know it used to be the condemned cell. There's a name carved on the window-sill, and a date in ninety-eight—I can't—I can't remember the name.'

'Was there any one accused, Max?' Una asked. 'Any record of a boy?'

Max frowned: 'Not that I remember—but so many were suspect—it's likely enough—poor boy!'

'I never could find out,' said Liam. 'Of course I wasn't far off delirium. It may have been hallucination or a dream.'

I did not believe he believed that and looked at him. He smiled.

'I want you to write it for me,' he pleaded quietly. 'I promised, you see.'

8

ELIZABETH BOWEN

The Happy Autumn Fields

The family walking party, though it comprised so many, did not deploy or straggle over the stubble but kept in a procession of threes and twos. Papa, who carried his Alpine stick, led, flanked by Constance and little Arthur. Robert and Cousin Theodore, locked in studious talk, had Emily attached but not quite abreast. Next came Digby and Lucius, taking, to left and right, imaginary aim at rooks. Henrietta and Sarah brought up the rear.

It was Sarah who saw the others ahead on the blond stubble, who knew them, knew what they were to each other, knew their names and knew her own. It was she who felt the stubble under her feet, and who heard it give beneath the tread of the others a continuous different more distant soft stiff scrunch. The field and all these out-lying fields in view knew as Sarah knew that they were Papa's. The harvest had been good and was now in: he was satisfied—for this afternoon he had made the instinctive choice of his most womanly daughter, most nearly infant son. Arthur, whose hand Papa was holding, took an anxious hop, a skip and a jump to every stride of the great man's. As for Constance—Sarah could often see the flash of her hat-feather as she turned her head, the curve of her close bodice as she turned her torso. Constance gave Papa her attention but not her thoughts, for she had already been sought in marriage.

The landowners' daughters, from Constance down, walked with their beetle-green, mole or maroon skirts gathered up and carried clear of the ground, but for Henrietta, who was still ankle-free. They walked inside a continuous stuffy sound, but left silence behind them. Behind them, rooks that had risen and circled, sun striking blue from their blue-black wings, planed one by one to the earth and settled to peck again. Papa and the boys were dark-clad as the rooks but with no sheen, but for their white collars.

It was Sarah who located the thoughts of Constance, knew what a twisting prisoner was Arthur's hand, felt to the depths of Emily's pique at Cousin Theodore's inattention, rejoiced with Digby and Lucius at the imaginary fall of so many rooks. She fell back, however, as from a rocky range, from the converse of Robert and Cousin Theodore. Most she knew that she swam with love at the nearness of Henrietta's young and alert face and eyes which shone with the sky and queried the afternoon.

She recognized the colour of valediction, tasted sweet sadness, while from the cottage inside the screen of trees wood-smoke rose melting pungent and blue. This was the eve of the brothers' return to school. It was like a Sunday; Papa had kept the late afternoon free; all (all but one) encircling Robert, Digby, and Lucius, they walked the estate the brothers would not see again for so long. Robert, it could be felt, was not unwilling to return to his books; next year he would go to college like Theodore; besides, to all this they saw he was not the heir. But in Digby and Lucius aiming and popping hid a bodily grief, the repugnance of victims, though these two were further from being heirs than Robert.

Sarah said to Henrietta: 'To think they will not be here tomorrow!'

'*Is* that what you are thinking about?' Henrietta asked, with her subtle taste for the truth.

'More, I was thinking that you and I will be back again by one another at table. . . .'

'You know we are always sad when the boys are going, but we are never sad when the boys have gone.' The sweet reciprocal guilty smile that started on Henrietta's lips finished on those of Sarah. 'Also,' the young sister said, 'we know this is only something happening again. It happened last year, and it will happen next. But oh how should I feel, and how should you feel, if it were something that had not happened before?'

'For instance, when Constance goes to be married?'

'Oh, I don't mean *Constance!*' said Henrietta.

'So long,' said Sarah, considering, 'as, whatever it is, it happens to both of us?' She must never have to wake in the early morning except to the birdlike stirrings of Henrietta, or have her cheek brushed in the dark by the frill of another pillow in whose hollow did not repose Henrietta's cheek. Rather than they should cease to lie in the same bed she prayed they might lie in the same grave. 'You and I will stay as we are,' she said, 'then nothing can touch one without touching the other.'

'So you say; so I hear you say!' exclaimed Henrietta, who then, lips apart, sent Sarah her most tormenting look. 'But I cannot forget that you chose to be born without me; that you would not wait—' But here she broke off, laughed outright and said: 'Oh, *see!*'

Ahead of them there had been a dislocation. Emily took advantage of having gained the ridge to kneel down to tie her bootlace so abruptly that Digby all but fell over her, with an exclamation. Cousin Theodore had been civil enough to pause beside Emily, but Robert, lost to all but what he was saying, strode on, head down, only just not colliding into Papa and Constance, who had turned to look back. Papa, astounded, let go of Arthur's hand, whereupon Arthur fell flat on the stubble.

'Dear me,' said the affronted Constance to Robert.

Papa said: 'What is the matter there? May I ask, Robert, where you are going, sir? Digby, remember that is your sister Emily.'

'Cousin Emily is in trouble,' said Cousin Theodore.

Poor Emily, telescoped in her skirts and by now scarlet under her hatbrim, said in a muffled voice: 'It is just my bootlace, Papa.'

'Your bootlace, Emily?'

'I was just tying it.'

'Then you had better tie it.—Am I to think,' said Papa, looking round them all, 'that you must all go down like a pack of ninepins because Emily has occasion to stoop?'

At this Henrietta uttered a little whoop, flung her arms round Sarah, buried her face in her sister and fairly suffered with laughter. She could contain this no longer; she shook all over. Papa, who found Henrietta so hopelessly out of order that he took no notice of her except at table, took no notice, simply giving the signal for the others to collect themselves and move on. Cousin Theodore, helping Emily to her feet, could be seen to see how her heightened colour became her, but she dispensed with his hand chillily, looked elsewhere, touched the brooch at her throat and said: 'Thank you, I have not sustained an accident.' Digby apologized to Emily, Robert to Papa and Constance. Constance righted Arthur, flicking his breeches over with her handkerchief. All fell into their different steps and resumed their way.

Sarah, with no idea how to console laughter, coaxed, 'Come, come, come,' into Henrietta's ear. Between the girls and the others the distance widened; it began to seem that they would be left alone.

'And why not?' said Henrietta, lifting her head in answer to Sarah's thought.

They looked around them with the same eyes. The shorn uplands seemed to float on the distance, which extended dazzling to tiny blue glassy hills. There was no end to the afternoon, whose light went on ripening now they had scythed the corn. Light filled the silence which, now Papa and the others were out of hearing, was complete. Only screens of trees intersected and knolls made islands in the vast fields. The mansion and the home farm had sunk for ever below them in the expanse of woods, so that hardly a ripple showed where the girls dwelled.

The shadow of the same rook circling passed over Sarah then over Henrietta, who in their turn cast one shadow across the stubble. 'But, Henrietta, we cannot stay here for ever.'

Henrietta immediately turned her eyes to the only lonely plume of smoke, from the cottage. 'Then let us go and visit the poor old man. He is dying and the others are happy. One day we shall pass and see no more smoke; then soon his roof will fall in, and we shall always be sorry we did not go today.'

'But he no longer remembers us any longer.'

'All the same, he will feel us there in the door.'

'But can we forget this is Robert's and Digby's and Lucius's goodbye walk? It would be heartless of both of us to neglect them.'

'Then how heartless Fitzgeorge is!' smiled Henrietta.

'Fitzgeorge is himself, the eldest and in the Army. Fitzgeorge I'm afraid is not an excuse for us.'

A resigned sigh, or perhaps the pretence of one, heaved up Henrietta's still narrow bosom. To delay matters for just a moment more she shaded her eyes with one hand, to search the distance like a sailor looking for a sail. She gazed with hope and zeal in every direction but that in which she and Sarah were bound to go. Then—'Oh, but Sarah, here *they* are, coming—they are!' she cried. She brought out her handkerchief and began to fly it, drawing it to and fro through the windless air.

In the glass of the distance, two horsemen came into view, cantering on a grass track between the fields. When the track dropped into a hollow they dropped with it, but by now the drumming of hoofs was heard. The reverberation filled the land, the silence and Sarah's being; not watching for the riders to reappear she instead fixed her eyes on her sister's handkerchief which, let hang limp while its owner intently waited, showed a bitten corner as well as a damson stain. Again it became a flag, in furious motion.—'Wave too, Sarah, wave too! Make your bracelet flash!'

'They must have seen us if they will ever see us,' said Sarah, standing still as a stone.

Henrietta's waving at once ceased. Facing her sister she crunched up her handkerchief, as though to stop it acting a lie. 'I can see you are shy,' she said in a dead voice. 'So shy you won't even wave to *Fitzgeorge*?'

Her way of not speaking the *other* name had a hundred meanings; she drove them all in by the way she did not look at Sarah's face. The impulsive breath she had caught stole silently out again, while her eyes—till now at their brightest, their most speaking—dulled with uncomprehending solitary alarm. The ordeal of awaiting Eugene's approach thus became for Sarah, from moment to moment, torture.

Fitzgeorge, Papa's heir, and his friend Eugene, the young neighbouring squire, struck off the track and rode up at a trot with their hats doffed. Sun striking low turned Fitzgeorge's flesh to coral and made Eugene blink his dark eyes. The young men reined in; the girls looked up the horses. 'And my father, Constance, the others?' Fitzgeorge demanded, as though the stubble had swallowed them.

'Ahead, on the way to the quarry, the other side of the hill.'

'We heard you were all walking together,' Fitzgeorge said, seeming dissatisfied.

'We are following.'

'What, alone?' said Eugene, speaking for the first time.

'Forlorn!' glittered Henrietta, raising two mocking hands.

Fitzgeorge considered, said 'Good' severely, and signified to Eugene that they would ride on. But too late: Eugene had dismounted. Fitzgeorge saw, shrugged and flicked his horse to a trot; but Eugene led his slowly between the sisters. Or rather, Sarah walked on his left hand, the horse on his right and Henrietta the other side of the horse. Henrietta, acting like somebody quite alone, looked up at the sky, idly holding one of the empty stirrups. Sarah, however, looked at the ground, with Eugene inclined as though to speak but not speaking. Enfolded, dizzied, blinded as though inside a wave, she could feel his features carved in brightness above her. Alongside the slender stepping of his horse, Eugene matched his naturally long free step to hers. His elbow was through the reins; with his fingers he brushed back the lock that his bending to her had sent falling over his forehead. She recorded the sublime act and knew what smile shaped his lips. So each without looking trembled before an image, while slow colour burned up the curves of her cheeks. The consummation would be when their eyes met.

At the other side of the horse, Henrietta began to sing. At once her pain, like a scientific ray, passed through the horse and Eugene to penetrate Sarah's heart.

We surmount the skyline: the family come into our view, we into theirs. They are halted, waiting, on the decline to the quarry. The handsome statufied group in strong yellow sunshine, aligned by Papa and crowned by Fitzgeorge, turn their judging eyes on the laggards, waiting to close their ranks round Henrietta and Sarah and Eugene. One more moment and it will be too late; no further communication will be possible. Stop oh stop Henrietta's heart-breaking singing! Embrace her close again! Speak the only possible word! Say—oh, say what? Oh, the word is lost!

'Henrietta . . .'

A shock of striking pain in the knuckles of the outflung hand—Sarah's? The eyes, opening, saw that the hand had struck, not been struck: there was a corner of a table. Dust, whitish and gritty, lay on the top of the table and on the telephone. Dull but piercing white light filled the room and what was left of the ceiling; her first thought was that it must have snowed. If so, it was winter now.

Through the calico stretched and tacked over the window came the sound of a piano: someone was playing Tchaikowosky badly in a room without windows or doors. From somewhere else in the hollowness came a cascade of hammering. Close up, a voice: 'Oh, *awake*, Mary?' It came from the other side of the open door, which jutted out between herself and the speaker—he on the threshold, she lying on the uncovered mattress of a bed. The speaker added: 'I had been going away.'

Summoning words from somewhere she said: 'Why? I didn't know you were here.'

'Evidently—Say, who is "Henrietta"?'

Despairing tears filled her eyes. She drew back her hurt hand, began to suck at the knuckle and whimpered, 'I've hurt myself'.

A man she knew to be 'Travis', but failed to focus, came round the door saying: 'Really I don't wonder.' Sitting down on the edge of the mattress he drew her hand away from her lips and held it: the act, in itself gentle, was accompanied by an almost hostile stare of concern. 'Do listen, Mary,' he said. 'While you've slept I've been all over the house again, and I'm less than ever satisfied that it's safe. In your normal senses you'd never attempt to stay here. There've been alerts, and more than alerts, all day; one more bang anywhere near, which may happen at any moment, could bring the rest of this down. You keep telling me that you have things to see to—but do you know what chaos the rooms are in? Till they've gone ahead with more clearing, where can you hope to start? And if there *were*

89

anything you could do, you couldn't do it. Your own nerves know that, if you don't: it was almost frightening, when I looked in just now, to see the way you were sleeping—you've shut up shop.'

She lay staring over his shoulder at the calico window. He went on: 'You don't like it here. Your self doesn't like it. Your will keeps driving your self, but it can't be driven the whole way—it makes its own get-out: sleep. Well, I want you to sleep as much as you (really) do. But *not* here. So I've taken a room for you in a hotel; I'm going now for a taxi; you can practically make the move without waking up.'

'No, I can't get into a taxi without waking.'

'Do you realize you're the last soul left in the terrace?'

'Then who is that playing the piano?'

'Oh, one of the furniture-movers in Number Six. I didn't count the jaquerie; of course *they're* in possession—unsupervised, teeming, having a high old time. While I looked in on you in here ten minutes ago they were smashing out that conservatory at the other end. Glass being done in in cold blood—it was brutalizing. You never batted an eyelid; in fact, I thought you smiled.' He listened. 'Yes, the piano—they are highbrow all right. You know there's a workman downstairs lying on your blue sofa looking for pictures in one of your French books?'

'No,' she said, 'I've no idea who is there.'

'Obviously. With the lock blown off your front door anyone who likes can get in and out.'

'Including you.'

'Yes. I've had a word with a chap about getting that lock back before tonight. As for you, you don't know what is happening.'

'I did,' she said, locking her fingers before her eyes.

The unreality of this room and of Travis's presence preyed on her as figments of dreams that one knows to be dreams can do. This environment's being in semi-ruin struck her less than its being some sort of device or trap; and she rejoiced, if anything, in its decrepitude. As for Travis, he had his own part in the conspiracy to keep her from the beloved two. She felt he began to feel he was now unmeaning. She was struggling not to contemn him, scorn him for his ignorance of Henrietta, Eugene, her loss. His possessive angry fondness was part, of course, of the story of him and Mary, which like a book once read she remembered clearly but with indifference. Frantic at being delayed here, while the moment awaited her in the cornfield, she all but afforded a smile at the grotesquerie of being saddled with Mary's body and lover. Rearing up her head from the bare pillow, she looked, as far as the crossed feet, along the form inside which she found herself trapped: the irrelevant body of Mary, weighted down to the bed, wore a short black modern dress, flaked with plaster. The toes of the black suède shoes by their sickly whiteness showed Mary must have climbed over fallen ceilings; dirt engraved the fate-lines in Mary's palms.

This inspired her to say: 'But I've made a start; I've been pulling out things of value or things I want.'

For answer Travis turned to look down, expressively, at some object out of her sight, on the floor close by the bed. '*I* see,' he said, 'a musty old leather box gaping open with God knows what— junk, illegible letters, diaries, yellow photographs, chiefly plaster and dust. Of all things, Mary!—after a missing will?'

'Everything one unburies seems the same age.'

'Then what are these, where do they come from—family stuff?'

'No idea,' she yawned into Mary's hand. 'They may not even be mine. Having a house like this that had empty rooms must have made me store more than I knew, for years. I came on these, so I wondered. Look if you like.'

He bent and began to go through the box—it seemed to her, not unsuspiciously. While he blew grit off packets and fumbled with tapes she lay staring at the exposed laths of the ceiling, calculating. She then said: 'Sorry if I've been cranky, about the hotel and all. Go away just for two hours, then come back with a taxi, and I'll go quiet. Will that do?'

'Fine—except why not now?'

'*Travis* . . .'

'Sorry. It shall be as you say . . . You've got some good morbid stuff in this box, Mary—so far as I can see at a glance. The photographs seem more your sort of thing. Comic but lyrical. All of one set of people—a beard, a gun and a pot hat, a schoolboy with a moustache, a phaeton drawn up in front of a mansion, a group on steps, a *carte de visite* of two young ladies hand-in-hand in front of a painted field——'

'*Give that to me!*'

She instinctively tried, and failed, to unbutton the bosom of Mary's dress: it offered no hospitality to the photograph. So she could only fling herself over on the mattress, away from Travis, covering the two faces with her body. Racked by that oblique look of Henrietta's she recorded, too, a sort of personal shock at having seen Sarah for the first time.

Travis's hand came over her, and she shuddered. Wounded, he said: 'Mary . . .'

'Can't you leave *me* alone?'

She did not move or look till he had gone out saying: 'Then, in two hours.' She did not therefore see him pick up the dangerous box, which he took away under his arm, out of her reach.

They were back. Now the sun was setting behind the trees, but its rays passed dazzling between the branches into the beautiful warm red room. The tips of the ferns in the jardiniere curled gold, and Sarah, standing by the jardiniere, pinched at a leaf of scented geranium. The carpet had a great centre wreath of pomegranates, on which no tables or chairs stood, and its whole circle was between herself and the others.

No fire was lit yet, but where they were grouped was a hearth. Henrietta sat on a low stool, resting her elbow above her head on the arm of Mamma's chair, looking away intently as though into a fire, idle. Mamma embroidered, her needle slowed down by her thoughts; the length of tatting with roses she had already done overflowed stiffly over her supple skirts. Stretched on the rug at Mamma's feet, Arthur looked through an album of Swiss views, not liking them but vowed to be very quiet. Sarah, from where she stood, saw fuming cateracts and null eternal snows as poor Arthur kept turning over the pages, which had tissue paper between.

Against the white marble mantelpiece stood Eugene. The dark red shadows gathering in the drawing-room as the trees drowned more and more of the sun would reach him last, perhaps never: it seemed to Sarah that a lamp was lighted behind his face. He was the only gentleman with the ladies: Fitzgeorge had gone to the stables, Papa to give an order; Cousin Theodore was consulting a dictionary; in the gunroom Robert, Lucius, and Digby went through the sad rites, putting away their guns. All this was known to go on but none of it could be heard.

This particular hour of subtle light—not to be fixed by the clock, for it was early in winter and late in summer and in spring and autumn now, about Arthur's bedtime—had always, for Sarah, been Henrietta's. To be with her indoors or out, upstairs or down, was to share the same crepitation. Her spirit ran on past yours with a laughing shiver into an element of its own. Leaves and branches and mirrors in empty rooms became animate. The sisters rustled and scampered and concealed themselves where nobody else was in play that was full of fear, fear that was full of play. Till, by dint of making each other's hearts beat violently, Henrietta so wholly and Sarah so nearly lost all human reason that Mamma had been known to look at them searchingly as she sat instated for evening among the calm amber lamps.

But now Henrietta had locked the hour inside her breast. By spending it seated beside Mamma, in young imitation of Constance the Society daughter, she disclaimed for ever anything else. It had always been she who with one fierce act destroyed any toy that might be outgrown. She sat with straight back, poising her cheek remotely against her finger. Only by never looking at Sarah did she admit their eternal loss.

Eugene, not long returned from a foreign tour, spoke of travel, addressing himself to Mamma, who thought but did not speak of her wedding journey. But every now and then she had to ask Henrietta to pass the scissors or tray of carded wools, and Eugene seized every such moment to look at Sarah. Into eyes always brilliant with melancholy he dared begin to allow no other expression. But this in itself declared the conspiracy of still undeclared love.

For her part she looked at him as though he, transfigured by the strange light, were indeed a picture, a picture who could not see her. The wallpaper now flamed scarlet behind his shoulder. Mamma, Henrietta, even unknowing Arthur were in no hurry to raise their heads.

Henrietta said: 'If I were a man I should take my bride to Italy.'

'There are mules in Switzerland,' said Arthur.

'Sarah,' said Mamma, who turned in her chair mildly, 'where are you, my love; do you never mean to sit down?'

'To Naples,' said Henrietta.

'Are you not thinking of Venice?' said Eugene.

'No,' returned Henrietta, 'why should I be? I should like to climb the volcano. But then I am not a man, and am still less likely ever to be a bride.'

'Arthur . . .' Mamma said.

'Mamma?'

'Look at the clock.'

Arthur sighed politely, got up and replaced the album on the circular table, balanced upon the rest. He offered his hand to Eugene, his cheek to Henrietta and to Mamma; then he started towards Sarah, who came to meet him. 'Tell me, Arthur,' she said, embracing him, 'what did you do today?'

Arthur only stared with his button blue eyes. 'You were there too; we went for a walk in the cornfield, with Fitzgeorge on his horse, and I fell down.' He pulled out of her arms and said: 'I must go back to my beetle.' He had difficulty, as always, in turning the handle of the mahogany door. Mamma waited till he had left the room, then said: 'Arthur is quite a man now; he no longer comes running to me when he has hurt himself. Why, I did not even know he had fallen down. Before we know, he will be going away to school too.' She sighed and lifted her eyes to Eugene. 'Tomorrow is to be a sad day.'

Eugene with a gesture signified his own sorrow. The sentiments of Mamma could have been uttered only here in the drawing-room, which for all its size and formality was lyrical and almost exotic. There was a look like velvet in darker parts of the air; sombre window draperies let out gushes of lace; the music on the pianoforte bore tender titles, and the harp though unplayed gleamed in a corner, beyond sofas, whatnots, armchairs, occasional tables that all stood on tottering little feet. At any moment a tinkle might have been struck from the lustres' drops of the brighter day, a vibration from the musical instruments, or a quiver from the fringes and ferns. But the towering vases upon the consoles, the albums piled on the tables, the shells and figurines on the flights of brackets, all had, like the alabaster Leaning Tower of Pisa, an equilibrium of their own. Nothing would fall or change. And everything in the drawing-room was muted, weighted, pivoted by Mamma. When she added: 'We shall not feel quite the same,' it was to be understood that she would not have spoken thus from her place at the opposite end of Papa's table.

'Sarah,' said Henrietta curiously, 'what made you ask Arthur what he had been doing? Surely you have not forgotten today?'

The sisters were seldom known to address or question one another in public; it was taken that they knew each other's minds. Mamma, though untroubled, looked from one to the other. Henrietta continued: 'No day, least of all today, is like any other— Surely that must be true?' she said to Eugene. 'You will never forget my waving my handkerchief?'

Before Eugene had composed an answer, she turned to Sarah: 'Or *you*, them riding across the fields?'

Eugene also slowly turned his eyes on Sarah, as though awaiting with something like dread her answer to the question he had not asked. She drew a light little gold chair into the middle of the wreath of the carpet, where no one ever sat, and sat down. She said: 'But since then I think I have been asleep.'

'Charles the First walked and talked half an hour after his head was cut off,' said Henrietta mockingly. Sarah in anguish pressed the palms of her hands together upon a shred of geranium leaf.

'How else,' she said, 'could I have had such a bad dream?'

'That must be the explanation!' said Henrietta.

'A trifle fanciful,' said Mamma.

However rash it might be to speak at all, Sarah wished she knew how to speak more clearly. The obscurity and loneliness of her trouble was not to be borne. How could she put into words the feeling of dislocation, the formless dread that had been with her since she found herself in the drawing-room? The source of both had been what she must call her dream. How could she tell the others with what vehemence she tried to attach her being to each second, not because each was singular in itself, each a drop condensed from the mist of love in the room, but because she apprehended that the seconds were numbered? Her hope was that the others at least half knew. Were Henrietta and Eugene able to understand how completely, how nearly for ever, she had been swept from them, would they not without fail each grasp one of her hands?—She went so far as to throw her hands out, as though alarmed by a wasp. The shred of geranium fell to the carpet.

Mamma, tracing this behaviour of Sarah's to only one cause, could not but think reproachfully of Eugene. Delightful as his conversation had been, he would have done better had he paid this call with the object of interviewing Papa. Turning to Henrietta she asked her to ring for the lamps, as the sun had set.

Eugene, no longer where he had stood, was able to make no gesture towards the bell-rope. His dark head was under the tide of dusk; for, down on one knee on the edge of the wreath, he was feeling over the carpet for what had fallen from Sarah's hand. In the inevitable silence rooks on the return from the fields could be heard streaming over the house; their sound filled the sky and even the room, and it appeared so useless to ring the bell that Henrietta stayed quivering by Mamma's chair. Eugene rose, brought out his fine white handkerchief and, while they watched, enfolded carefully in it what he had just found, then returning the handkerchief to his breast pocket. This was done so deep in the reverie that accompanies any final act that Mamma instinctively murmured to Henrietta: 'But you will be my child when Arthur has gone.'

The door opened for Constance to appear on the threshold. Behind her queenly figure globes approached, swimming in their own light: these were the lamps for which Henrietta had not rung, but these first were put on the hall tables. 'Why, Mamma,' exclaimed Constance, 'I cannot see who is with you!'

'Eugene is with us,' said Henrietta, 'but on the point of asking if he may send for his horse.'

'Indeed?' said Constance to Eugene. 'Fitzgeorge has been asking for you, but I cannot tell where he is now.'

The figures of Emily, Lucius, and Cousin Theodore criss-crossed the lamplight there in the hall, to mass behind Constance's in the drawing-room door. Emily, over her sister's shoulder, said: 'Mamma, Lucius wishes to ask you whether for once he may take his guitar to school.'—'One objection, however,' said Cousin Theodore, 'is that Lucius's trunk is already locked and strapped.' 'Since Robert is taking his box of inks,' said Lucius, 'I do not see why I should not take my guitar.'—'But Robert,' said Constance, 'will soon be going to college.'

Lucius squeezed past the others into the drawing-room in order to look anxiously at Mamma, who said: 'You have thought of this late; we must go and see.' The others parted to let Mamma, followed by Lucius, out. Then Constance, Emily, and Cousin Theodore deployed and sat down in different parts of the drawing-room, to await the lamps.

'I am glad the rooks have done passing over,' said Emily, 'they make me nervous.'—'Why?' yawned Constance haughtily, 'what do you think could happen?' Robert and Digby silently came in.

Eugene said to Sarah: 'I shall be back tomorrow.'

'But, oh—' she began. She turned to cry: 'Henrietta!'

'Why, what is the matter?' said Henrietta, unseen at the back of the gold chair. 'What could be sooner than tomorrow?'

'But something terrible may be going to happen.'

'There cannot fail to be tomorrow,' said Eugene gravely.

'*I* will see that there is tomorrow,' said Henrietta.

'You will never let me out of your sight?'

Eugene, addressing himself to Henrietta, said: 'Yes, promise her what she asks.'

Henrietta cried: 'She *is* never out of my sight. Who are you to ask me that, you Eugene? Whatever tries to come between me and Sarah becomes nothing. Yes, come tomorrow, come sooner, come—when you like, but no one will ever be quite alone with

Sarah. You do not even know what you are trying to do. It is *you* who are making something terrible happen.—Sarah, tell him that that is true! Sarah——'

The others, in the dark on the chairs and sofas, could be felt to turn their judging eyes upon Sarah, who, as once before, could not speak—

—The house rocked: simultaneously the calico window split and more ceiling fell, though not on the bed. The enormous dull sound of the explosion died, leaving a minor trickle of dissolution still to be heard in parts of the house. Until the choking stinging plaster dust had had time to settle, she lay with lips pressed close, nostrils not breathing and eyes shut. Remembering the box, Mary wondered if it had been again buried. No, she found, looking over the edge of the bed: that had been unable to happen because the box was missing. Travis, who must have taken it, would when he came back no doubt explain why. She looked at her watch, which had stopped, which was not surprising; she did not remember winding it for the last two days, but then she could not remember much. Through the torn window appeared the timelessness of an impermeably clouded late summer afternoon.

There being nothing left, she wished he would come to take her to the hotel. The one way back to the fields was barred by Mary's surviving the fall of ceiling. Sarah was right in doubting that there would be tomorrow: Eugene, Henrietta were lost in time to the woman weeping there on the bed, no longer reckoning who she was.

At last she heard the taxi, then Travis hurrying up the littered stairs. 'Mary, you're all right, Mary—*another*?' Such a helpless white face came round the door that she could only hold out her arms and say: 'Yes, but where have *you* been?'

'You said two hours. But I wish——'

'I have missed you.'

'Have you? Do you know you are crying?'

'Yes. How are we to live without natures? We only know inconvenience now, not sorrow. Everything pulverizes so easily because it is rot-dry; one can only wonder that it makes so much noise. The source, the sap must have dried up, or the pulse must have stopped, before you and I were conceived. So much flowed through people; so little flows through us. All we can do is imitate love or sorrow.— Why did you take away my box?'

He only said: 'It is in my office.'

She continued: 'What has happened is cruel: I am left with a fragment torn out of a day, a day I don't even know where or when; and now how am I to help laying that like a pattern against the poor stuff of everything else?—Alternatively, I am a person drained by a dream. I cannot forget the climate of those hours. Or life at that pitch, eventful—not happy, no, but strung like a harp. I have had a sister called Henrietta.'

'And I have been looking inside your box. What else can you expect?—I have had to write off this day, from the work point of view, thanks to you. So could I sit and do nothing for the last two hours? I just glanced through this and that—still, I know the family.'

'You said it was morbid stuff.'

'Did I? I still say it gives off something.'

She said: 'And then there was Eugene.'

'Probably. I don't think I came on much of his except some notes he must have made for Fitzgeorge from some book on scientific farming. Well, there it is: I have sorted everything out and put it back again, all but a lock of hair that tumbled out of a letter I could not trace. So I've got the hair in my pocket.'

'What colour is it?'

'Ash-brown. Of course, it is a bit—desiccated. Do you want it?'

'No,' she said with a shudder. 'Really, Travis, what revenges you take!'

'I didn't look at it that way,' he said puzzled.

'Is the taxi waiting?' Mary got off the bed and, picking her way across the room, began to look about for things she ought to take with her, now and then stopping to brush her dress. She took the mirror out of her bag to see how dirty her face was. 'Travis—' she said suddenly.

'Mary?'

'Only, I——'

'That's all right. Don't let us imitate anything just at present.'

In the taxi, looking out of the window, she said: 'I suppose, then, that I am descended from Sarah?'

'No,' he said, 'that would be impossible. There must be some reason why you should have those papers, but that is not the one. From all negative evidence Sarah, like Henrietta, remained unmarried. I found no mention of either, after a certain date, in the letters of Constance, Robert, or Emily, which makes it seem likely both died young. Fitzgeorge refers, in a letter to Robert written in his old age, to some friend of their youth who was thrown from his horse and killed, riding back after a visit to their home. The young man, whose name doesn't appear, was alone; and the evening, which was in autumn, was fine though late. Fitzgeorge wonders, and says he will always wonder, what made the horse shy in those empty fields.'

9

J. F. BYRNE

'Ghosts' in House on Cork Hill

Towards the end of 1902, a house on Cork Hill became vacant. This house was about 150 yards from the entrance to the Castle Yard. It stood almost directly opposite the City Hall, and next door to the 'Mail' office which was on the corner of Parliament Street. For a considerable time before this, my cousin Mary had entertained the idea of renting a house in a good business district; a house large enough to provide dwelling accommodation for the four of us, together with at least two rooms for her own church business, and also a floor, preferably on the street level, suitable to be sublet as a business office.

When Mary saw this vacant house on Cork Hill, she thought it was just what she was looking for, and having talked the matter over with the rest of us, we all decided that she and I should have a look at it. On enquiry, we learned that the owner of the house was one Walter Butler, who at that time was Dublin City Architect. Mary and I had a talk with Mr Butler in his residence, and he arranged to have a man meet us at the house at 9 a.m. the following morning and let us view it.

Next morning, Mary and I met a young man at the hall door of the house, and he let us in to see it. We found it was in very fair condition, but requiring, of course, the customary cleaning, painting, renovation of wallpaper, and some minor improvements. One thing we noticed, with very little concern more than thinking it odd, was that on the front of the mantelpiece in the top back room was written very prominently, in several places, the one word 'Ghosts'.

Altogether Mary and I spent nearly an hour inspecting the place, and making tentative plans how we would fix it up and settle in it. We decided that the ground floor should be sublet for an office, or offices; that the second floor should be the 'church warerooms'; that the top floor should be our living and sleeping quarters, and that we would cook and eat in the basement, where one of the rooms was fitted out as a comparatively comfortable kitchen.

While we were looking, cogitating, and planning, we twice heard the footsteps of other people, apparently, like ourselves, looking over the house, and we assumed that the owner had also arranged to let other prospective tenants view the place simultaneously with us. So when Mary and I, having concluded our inspection and planning, were taking leave of the young man who was standing at the open hall door, I said to him just for talk sake, 'You had other people in to look over the house; how do you think they liked it?' He answered with more emphasis than seemed to be required, 'Nobody entered this house since you went into it. I have stood here all the time without moving a step from this open hall door, and I have let nobody but you two into the place.'

Mary had two more interviews with Mr Butler, as a result of which he agreed to accept her as tenant on a monthly basis, but he refused to do any renovation or improvement in the house unless we would give him a full year's rent of sixty pounds in advance.

Well, after deliberating the project for a few days, we scraped together the required sixty pounds, which Mary gave in cash to Mr Butler. He in turn gave her a receipt, with a comprehensive memorandum of the whole transaction. He also gave her the keys of the house. In the early afternoon of the day on which this occurred, Mary went to the house to make a thorough final study of what she wanted done, and how she wanted it. While in the house alone, she again heard footsteps of people walking through it; these footsteps being especially loud on the stairs from the basement to the top. These noises were so real that she went down to the hall door to see whether she had inadvertently failed to close it properly. But the hall door was closed tight.

When she had finished her study of the house, Mary prepared to

come home, first making sure that the back door and any accessible windows were firmly closed. Then when she emerged from
the hall door, she turned and locked it carefully, and as she did so, a
man whom she had noticed for some time standing outside on the
footpath came over to her and said, 'Miss Fleming, I'd like to talk to
you.' Mary took in at a glance that this man was a decent fellow. He
seemed like a prosperous tradesman, of about her own age, and his
manner was gentlemanly. So when Mary nodded, 'Yes, you may,'
he said, 'You don't know me, ma'am, but I know you; for years ago
I was a friend of your Uncle Matt Byrne; and I want to advise you
that if you're thinking of taking this house here, don't do it. The
place is haunted. I know what I'm talking about—and it's not
hearsay.'

'But,' said Mary, 'I have already taken the house and got the
keys.'

'Well then, ma'am, all I can say is I'm terribly sorry. It was in the
basement of this very house here that the Invincibles used to meet
before the Phoenix Park murders. I saw them here myself, often
and often—James Carey, young Tim Kelly, Joe Brady, and the rest
of them. It's an awful pity you should have anything to do with a
house like this. But I wish ye all the luck in the world, and of course
I don't think very much wrong can happen to a good woman like
you.'

That night at dinner and later, we did not lack subjects for conversation and speculation. Mary was positive she had never before
met the man who had claimed friendship with my father; and she
was full of regret that, as she explained, she was so preoccupied
with their conversation, she never thought of asking him for, and
he did not give, either his name or address. Her description of him,
of his dress, appearance, manner and talk, was very detailed and
minute, but neither Cicely nor Emily could place him. About this I
said nothing, but I did reflect that there are more things in heaven
and earth than are to be found in anyone's philosophy.

On the morning of the day after, which was a Saturday, I went
round alone to the house, bringing along with me a candlestick,
candles, and wax matches. I went through the house, without a

microscope, it's true, but in much the same way as Sherlock Holmes might have done. In the whole house I saw nothing out of the ordinary except one thing, and that was in the west wall of the back kitchen in the basement. In this wall there was a recession, as if there had been a small opening into another smaller cellar, or apartment, or possibly, tunnel. This opening, into whatever had been there, or may have still been there, was about four and one-half feet high and about the same in width, but it was bricked up, and no attempt had ever been made to conceal this former opening; just the plain bricks and mortar, with no plaster or other covering.

In all other respects, so far as I saw, there was nothing in the house out of the ordinary; and moreover during the half-hour or so it took me to scrutinize the place from bottom to top, nothing out of the ordinary occurred. I decided then to postpone further investigation till that night. None of us had ever been in the house late at night, and I wanted to see what would happen; so I left the candlestick, candles, and a box of vestas just inside the hall door, which I locked carefully from the outside.

After dinner, I went to the National Library, carrying with me, as I occasionally did, a stout ashplant, which was one of several I had uprooted long before in Carrigmore. When the Library closed at about five minutes to ten, I walked from there with Paddy Merriman and Skeffington to the entrance to Trinity College on College Green. Here I said good-night to my two companions and walked straight west on Dame Street to the house on Cork Hill, which I entered at about ten fifteen.

When inside, I lit my candle, and locked and bolted the hall door. I then went once more through the house from bottom to top, giving special attention to the back door and to two windows in the back of the house which might have been accessible from outside. Then I continued up to the top floor of the house where I had decided to keep my vigil. Up here I put out my candle, afterwards trimming the wick by the light of a wax vesta, so that it could be relit quickly when required.

My purpose in putting out the candle was perhaps a little vague.

But I was of the firm opinion that the noises in the house were due to natural and not to spiritual causes. It was part of my thought that perhaps someone had found a way of getting into the house for some purpose or another and that if there was a light, he would be warned.

I stood there in the top front room of the house; but I was not completely in the dark. For through the two windows some light did enter the room from the tall electric arc-burner street lamps. It was very cold that night, but that didn't trouble me much because I was warmly clad, and with a frieze overcoat. I stood looking out of the windows watching the few vehicles and pedestrians outside, and noting the infrequent passing of the well-lit Inchicore trams. From time to time I looked at my watch, and as one tram climbed the hill on its way to Inchicore, I said to myself that must be the last tram tonight from Nelson's Pillar.

At this very moment, there arose, apparently from the basement, a sudden loud noise as of many persons tramping the kitchen floor and up the stairway to the hall. It was but the work of an instant for me to take off my cumbersome overcoat; throw it on the floor between the two windows; hang my ash plant by its crook over my left forearm; seize the candlestick with candle and vestas, and go out to the top lobby.

At this point, standing still in the darkness, the din of the scuffle in the basement was much louder, and for perhaps thirty seconds continued unabated. Then suddenly I heard a thud which seemed to shake the whole house to its foundations, and this thud was followed immediately by the sound of heavy bumping on the stairway from the hall to the basement. Then, after a complete silence for about ten seconds, there was the sound of a heavy footstep mounting the first flight of stairs up from the hall. These footsteps continued slowly but heavily up to the first lobby directly beneath me.

When the footsteps continued to ascend, I lit my vesta, which gave nearly as much light as would the candle, and looked over the horizontal balustrade to the flight immediately below, but there was no one in sight. I then applied my burning vesta to the candle, the while the footsteps reached the top landing and were coming up the last flight to the lobby on which I stood.

Holding my candlestick in my left hand I grasped my ashplant near its ferrule, with the intention of laying about with its sturdy crook, but this I remembered from experience was no way to handle my stick because it would give my adversary a chance to grab it by the crook and pull it away from me. So I let my stick drop in my fist till I grasped the crook, and meanwhile the heavy steps continued till they sounded right beside me on the lobby where I stood, and then they passed through the open door into the top back room. Instantly I followed, but there was nothing out of place in the room, and I found myself standing there, with my lit candle in my left hand and my ashplant in my right, alone in utter silence. The sound of the footsteps had ceased.

This was a small room, about thirteen feet square, and for perhaps five seconds I stood still in its centre, listening. But there was no sound. Then I swished my ashplant, this way and that, all round the room, but it encountered nothing. Looking towards the mantelpiece I observed the word 'Ghosts' splattered over it, and at the sight of this I became incensed. I stepped over and slashed viciously with my ashplant on the many places where the word was written, as if in slashing at the word I was slashing at the thing it connoted.

Suddenly I realized what I was doing and I was mortified. I recalled in a flash the soliloquy of Hamlet, in which he berates himself that he should 'fall a-cursing, like a very drab, a scullion'. I had not fallen a-cursing in words, but the futile whacks of my plant were an outward manifestation of exactly the same mood which the Dane decried, and my principal feelings became at once both shame and disgust.

I left the room without further ado, went into the front room, put on my overcoat, descended to the hall and then to the cellar, looking rather perfunctorily to see if there was anything untoward. There wasn't anything out of the way, as I knew well there wouldn't be. And then I stepped out of the house into the bleak night and a deserted street. That night and early morning I walked out to Rathfarnham by way of Harold's Cross, returning through

Rathmines. I turned into Harcourt Street and around Stephen's Green, and then home. I wanted to make up my mind what was best to do.

None of us spoke about the matter that day until, as we sat around after dinner, I brought the matter swiftly to a head by saying that I had decided we should not move into the house. I narrated very briefly and without detail my visit of the preceding night. I made it clear that, speaking for my part, I hated to come to this decision, but that there was nothing else for us to do but stay out.

Cicely was the first of the female trinity to say anything, and then, flicking a couple of non-existent crumbs on the tablecloth, she countered with, 'Oh, that's all rubbish. Maybe there is noise in the place, and maybe there isn't—maybe it comes from outside— next door, or somewhere, and anyway even if there is something in the place, we can hang relics around and sprinkle holy water everywhere, and then we'll be safe.' I had known perfectly well that this would be Cicely's reaction. The whole realm of her religion was fortressed on the North, South, East, and West, by holy water, relics, miraculous medals, and scapulars, with an occasional agnus dei scattered strategically here and there like pillboxes round a frontier. But if Cicely were in the house and anything took place she'd go tottering round the room woebegone and helpless, mooning and moaning and mumbling, 'Oh, Mhuire 's truagh— Mhuire 's truagh, what's goin' to become of us, at all, at all!'

As for Emily, she said nothing; but I knew from the look of relief on her face that she thoroughly agreed with me. And then the very practical Mary said, 'What about our sixty pounds? We'll never get that back.' 'No,' I admitted, 'I don't think there's the slightest chance of that, but you and I can go to Mr Butler in his office first thing in the morning, and see what he'll do about it.'

Well, we went to Mr Butler, but he wasn't in his office, so we didn't see him until that evening in his home. When Mary told him she had changed her mind about taking the place and why, I could see that he wasn't a bit surprised. But he said he couldn't, and he didn't, give us any assurance about returning the money. Mary ended the interview by saying to him: 'Well, Mr Butler, I hope your conscience will be your guide as to what you ought to do. As for us, although we surely can't afford to lose that money, we don't want the house, so I'm giving you back the keys and washing my hands of the whole transaction.'

Now let me ask you, what would you have done, had you been in my place?

Well, we didn't go into the house; and we did forfeit our badly needed sixty pounds. So that was that—but it wasn't the end of it.

On the night of February 26–27, 1903, just a couple of months after these incidents, there occurred one of the heaviest storms to which Ireland has ever been subjected. Damage and ruin over the City of Dublin were widespread. It was during this storm that the world-famed Chesterfield elms—scores of them—along the main road of the Phoenix Park were uprooted and destroyed.

On Cork Hill, too, there was a sight of destruction. The house we had decided not to enter, and which was still unrented, stood in ruins. A chimney stack which had been blown down on its roof, had gone down to the basement, bringing down every floor in the house along with it.

10

SHANE LESLIE

A Laugh on the Professor

This is not my story but the Professor's, though he refuses to have a ghost story attached to his name and strongly disapproves the Society for Psychical Research.

In a way he would be a perfect subject for a supernormal manifestation, as he is precise, prosaic and, as this story passed in Ireland, it is better scientifically that he should be Protestant: but as he discounts all the miraculous he would be more easily termed Agnostic.

He returned to my old college at Cambridge one term, after a holi-day in Ireland. The district in which he had been entertained was familiar to me as my own County. I was interested to learn how he had fared when I wended to his room on A–Z staircase. Certainly his health had improved and I should say his nerve-power. For weeks he had not been sleeping well in college and I was pleased to hear that his first night in Ireland he had slept the clock round and had never missed a day's sport in consequence.

He was not a sportsman and therefore had enjoyed enormously the afternoons of rough snipe-shooting and even coarser fishing which were provided for him. I knew well those dissipations at which the professional turns up his nose. Only the bungling amateur can really enjoy the discomforts of Irish bogs and lakes in pursuit of snipe and pike—'the unshootable and the uneatable' as he described them to me with slight memory of a witticism of Oscar Wilde. That amusing Irishman had once paid our college a week-end visit and for years the staff invented Oscarisms.

One evening the Professor and myself found ourselves alone after consumption of much college coffee, which had inspired the rest of the company to disperse study-bent. The Professor poked his fire, extinguished the light and began to browse on his Irish memories. I had known his host well and indeed there was hardly a bog or a lake he recalled which I did not know better than himself. There was only one lake in the neighbourhood he had not fished and that was because his host for some reason disliked it.

He was prosaic as usual in the telling and I began to loll myself to sleep. I might say that, though a fine mathematician, he was a dull lecturer. I was weary of hearing about his tiny bags of snipe and absurdly lightweight monsters—he thought a ten-pound pike was worth stuffing for a glass case! I fell fast asleep and when I came slowly conscious he was still wagging along. He had turned to describe the pleasant and happy-go-lucky Irish life which has filled sketch books from Thackeray to anyone who has since cared to scribble the chatter of the inhabitants.

He had been surprised to find himself so comfortable and well-served in the castle occupied by his host, who had been ploughed several times in the Little Go but remained grateful to the Professor who had acted as his ineffectual coach—however, in Ireland examinations (as the civilized world will slowly discover) made little difference to life, certainly in the world outside the university.

My friend, his host, had returned to his demesnes, where Professors were as pleased to test his claret and snipe as they were apologetic for ploughing him till he could be ploughed no more. An excellent landlord, a sportsman and a gentleman without any initials tacked to his name or the imposition of a dead rabbit-skin by the Vice Chancellor, he remained an Irish gentleman.

Yes, the Professor said he had been very comfortable—such fine log-fires even in his bedroom—he didn't see much of the castle interior as they were out all day and too tired in the evenings except to stagger upstairs and dress for dinner—Yes they dressed in white shirts and ties like Oxford Dons—but laundry was cheap in Ireland and the water deliciously soft—servants were wonderful—he never saw the cook but he sent her a tip—there was a parlourmaid who waited at meals and he had tipped her and he remembered a third servant whom he had also left a tip for as he did not appear the day he left, a sort of superannuated footman he thought. They were wonderful servants. He preferred them to Cambridge 'bedders and gyps'. They did not show up much but everything possible was done—beds made—boots dried and cleaned and all the clothing neatly smoothed and laid out almost automatically (I have remarked how practical the Professor was). He seemed to forgive Ireland the economic sloth, impractical theories, and ludicrous inconveniences with which he had stuffed his mind before the visit. I was really bored, but the fire was still bright enough to whisk haunting glimmers and shadows round the room. There were famous draughts on A–Z staircase but I add, in case of arousing false expectation, that it was not the staircase which was rumoured to possess a ghost. I need not tell that story which has inspired Dr M. R. James with one of his most ghastly ghost-stories. Indeed, as it was a college ghost, it could never be published and I will not tell it now.

The Professor had taken a great liking to Irish servants and told it at length. I was pulling myself together to leave after he had expatiated on the virtues of the cook. What she could do with a snipe on toast or with a woodcock's trail—well I did not care—and I was out of my chair and moving to the door by the time he had told of his wonderful Irish 'bedder'—this housekeeper, parlour-maid, and housemaid all in one and she was only to be seen when she was wanted—just slipped about and had everything ready. He was glad he had handsomely tipped all three—all three—all three and my mind was slowly revolving his figures. I wanted to know how much he had left behind for he was not known as a ready sub-scriber to college funds. Yes, he had been generous to that paragon of domestics at his departure, the housekeeper: but the other two had been too modest to hang about the porch when his baggage was brought down. He had given the housekeeper a hand with his bags and then plunked down some sovereigns on the hall table (tips were done in gold currency in those days) and at the station he had asked his host to divide it amongst the rest—whereupon the old coachman respectfully pulled the cockade off his hat and said 'Thank you!' The Professor had not apparently reckoned on this as he felt his outdoor tips had been sufficiently concentrated on the gamekeeper. I must say the gamekeeper, who was a character called Hughey, would have been much worthier of this long fireside harangue.

However, I revolved in my mind the remarkable fact that the Professor had tipped three in the house: and by that time I had opened his door—'unsported his oak', should I say in college parlance, when some call in my memory began ringing a bell—like a burglar-bell in a top attic—there was something not right—I felt—in the Professor's arithmetic. He had tipped two in the field and three in the castle—he made out.

Well, I knew that castle and all its inhabitants but there should have been only two indoors to tip unless the garden boy or the underkeeper had been called in to help as sometimes when there was a party, but one Cambridge Professor does not make a party. I found myself reeling back into the armchair I had vacated and saying—'Tell me more—why were there three servants in the castle? There never were when I was staying there'—and I let him be loquacious. He continued, it was amazing how much work they did and how well. Every morning and evening all was done that a super-gyp the most accomplished of college servants could dream of doing—boots—fires—clothes laid out so well brushed and ready for instant use. The cooking was superb for game and even for vegetables, and that servant had remained invisible. He saw the housekeeper when required and the person he described as resembling 'a superannuated footman' even less. He met him sometimes on the stairs coming down or in the entry of his bedroom looking so earnest and stately that instinctively he had withdrawn against the panelling to let him pass. And there were his clothes perfectly laid and as often enough the housekeeper with a can of hot water which she deposited before quickly returning to the dining-room.

For the first time I was listening keenly and though I could not get him to start his memories afresh, I had the unconscious feeling (not from any logical sense of my own) that his story had something askew.

I questioned him about each of these perfect servants in turn to see how far they corresponded to my recent visits. He had begun retelling stories about old Hughey the keeper and I would have laughed aloud as Hughey swam back into memory. But for the moment Hughey was less interesting to me than 'the superannuated footman'. Somehow he did not make sense in my mind so I let the Professor talk on. Finally I broke out—'tell me more about that footman! Did he tell you wild stories like Hughey for the delectation of gentry? Did you converse with him agreeably as you say you did with the soft-voiced housekeeper?' Oh those voices which the Irish mists have melodified! I thought to myself.

No, he had not exchanged a word with the footman but he had been impressed by his old-fashioned livery and noiseless tread. And he told me again how he had often stood back out of his way in the corridor or as he left his bedroom. He was still drawling and did not observe how very interested I was. I held him to the tale that he enjoyed telling. He was clearly not accustomed to visiting a stately home or an Irish castle.

'I think I know the old livery he must have been wearing. Was it not a sort of old orange and dark green?'

'Yes, yes, and tarnished, very tarnished silver buttons as though they had been left out in the wet.'

I started at this. 'You certainly describe the family livery but it has not been worn for a long time, certainly not since I visited there in the Nineties. Are you sure of what you saw?'

'Of course I am.'

'Then why did you never speak to him?'

'Well he never said a word to me and I was generally in a hurry.'

'That did not strike you as strange?' He had stopped talking and I took up the tale 'Would you be worried if I told you that there was no footman serving all the time you were there?' There was silence at last.

'You would not believe me if I told you there had been a footman much as you describe, but he was never replaced after his demise.

He drowned himself in that lake your host did not like to fish. He was wearing the livery you describe when he was found. It is extraordinary that so precise an English Professor as you should be the first person to see him in a land where ghosts and ghost-seers are so common.'

There was little sleep on A–Z staircase that night for all the neighbours had to be roused and told the story and made to sign an account which was hastily written down as the Professor's true statement, though he objected like mad.

11

PETER SOMERVILLE-LARGE

Rich and Strange

Jack Colley's eldest child had known our daughter in playgroup years, then at school. They had been in and out of each other's houses, tongues orange from ice lollies, sharing roller-skates, bicycles, and felt pens. Deirdre came to our house more than Rachel went to hers; in winter we ran our central heating regularly and our place never smelt of nappies. They played upstairs or in the garden as weather dictates; they slumped over the same homework and skimped it to watch the children's programmes. Deirdre's cheeks bulged a little into her jaw like a bloodhound or a pear. Her flaxen hair was beginning to have dark streaks, and would end up mousy or dark brown. She had round eyes like one of her dolls, making her look surprised.

From time to time she brought over her sleeping-bag to spend the night, usually, it seemed, when she was about to acquire another sibling. On those occasions Jack and his aptly named Breda distributed their children among friends and relatives for the duration of Breda's stay at the Rotunda.

Relationships with the parents of children's friends have an element of gradual coercion. Our acquaintance with the Colleys progressed from shared school runs to female coffee mornings to formal entertainment to an exchange of small Christmas presents. In roughly the same time that the Black Death took to cross Asia and Europe, we found ourselves friends. Jack wasn't a bad fellow. He worked in local government, where his job, though not all that well paid, was inflation-proof and promised an adequate pension.

The boys had their names down for Gonzaga. He ran a big car, while Breda drove an ancient Morris Minor. Morris Minors have acquired a disreputable image, and tend to be driven by mountainy men or delinquent teenagers; but the Colleys' was grey and clean with a respectability that belonged to a previous decade. Both cars, like ours, were insured with the Private Motorists Protection Association. We didn't have all that much more in common.

For several summers running we took our holidays in rotation, since we lived in the same neighbourhood. In this way we could watch each other's houses and feed the other family's cat. The Colleys used to go abroad to some place like Benidorm or Lido di Jesolo, leaving behind a baby or two with Breda's mother. Then came the year when, like a lot of other people, they were kept at home by the falling pound. Jack bought a second-hand Sprite caravan and planned to take the whole family to Kerry. Breda's people came from there, and she had memories of holidays on relatives' farms.

Our holiday occurred first. We were back at the end of July, and a week later the Colleys made their ponderous departure, starting early in the morning. We waved from the bedroom as the Sprite passed, rattling over the concrete on its way towards the Limerick road.

That summer was exceptionally hot. In our suburb the long spell of glittering weather became a time to be endured. During August I escaped the office fairly often, and we drove to beaches south of the city. The Colleys sent us a postcard from Dingle with a picture of two currachs. But there were other things to think about besides the Colleys and after they returned we didn't see them until school began. The first days of September ended the hot weather abruptly so that the children went back in rain. On the Friday of the second week of September when I came home from work I found a sleeping-bag in the hall.

'Deirdre's staying,' Anne told me.

'What's wrong?'

'Breda's not well.'

'Miscarriage?'

Anne's voice took on the hush of scandal.

'A bit of a breakdown. Dr Byrne's sending her to the psychiatric unit at Elm Park. I feel terrible not having once seen them since they got back . . .'

'Will we be stuck with Deirdre for weeks?'

'Not at all. Only a couple of days. Breda's mother is coming up to take charge.'

'Poor old Jack. I'll give him a ring later on.' These things have become less embarrassing. In our suburb psychiatric troubles are more common than adultery.

'You won't get anything out of him.'

'I didn't mean that. I just feel sorry for the poor bastard.'

'All he would say when I asked him was that she was under a bit of stress.'

'Anyone who takes five children off in a caravan is looking for stress.'

In the end I left Jack and his troubles to himself. Over tea I noticed that the children were all in bad form. There was none of the usual giggling among the girls, no nudging or back-chat or teasing Tommy. In fact, hardly any conversation at all. I knew that Anne wanted to dump Deirdre about her mother, but there was something formidable about the child's reserve. I tried to ease things up with a few knock knock jokes and questions about school, and Miss Synott's boyfriend, a subject that usually promoted ribald laughter. Not a stir from either of them. Deirdre turned down her eyes like a propositioned nun.

Anne laid out her sleeping-bag as usual on our safari bed which was set up in Rachel's room. The girls didn't play or talk late. After midnight Deirdre woke us with screams. She couldn't remember, she said, when I asked, what the bad dream had been about.

Ten minutes after we had all settled down I found Rachel standing beside my bed.

'Go back to your room at once.'

'She's at it again.' We listened. We could hear her across the passage, not so loud, more like groans.

'The same silly word,' Rachel said.

As usual Anne had closed her eyes again with a determinedly

117

sleepy grunt. I have always been the one to get up and cope with the children. I put on my dressing-gown again and walked over into Rachel's room, half-lit by the light on the landing. Deirdre thrashed about in her sleeping-bag, muttering.

'Misericordia, miscericordia . . .'

'That's what she was saying before.'

Her face was covered with perspiration. I debated whether to wake her, when she solved the problem by waking herself.

'Another dream?' she nodded and put her thumb in her mouth. I went down to the kitchen to fetch a couple of mugs of hot milk, knowing that Rachel would insist on having one too. When I got back upstairs, both of them were lying quite silently in their respective beds. As I gave Deirdre two Junior Aspirin, I asked her. 'What's all this about misericordia? Is it a word that you hear in church?' Her upper lip, its line emphasized by a white moustache of milk, drew back like an angry cat. Her round eyes didn't have a look of surprise, but of terror.

'Never mind . . .' Rules were suspended, and I read aloud a soothing passage from *A Bear Named Paddington*. Then we went back to sleep. I remembered that Mass has been said in English for the past decade or so.

Next morning the girls seemed fine, as is so often the case after a wicked night, while Tommy had slept through it all. Anne wanted to drive to Superquinn for Saturday's big shopping. In the usual way we would have all gone together so that I could help with the bags of groceries and the children could spend their pocket money. But the rain was pouring down, and after all the excitements Anne and I both felt that it might be better if the children and I stayed at home and she managed on her own. The girls seemed indifferent while Tommy was persuaded with a promise of extra sweets. None of them really wanted to go out in the wet.

After I had washed the breakfast things I settled down in the kitchen with the paper. When the yells came from the playroom I only felt annoyance. They were of a type instantly recognizable, the unmistakable sounds of resentful children in unison making a noise like angry sheep.

'What's going on up there?' Rachel seemed to be siding with her brother, something I had hardly known her to do since the time Tommy began to speak. In the end I went storming upstairs.

Tommy keeps his Action Man meticulously, far better than Rachel maintains her dolls. His model has a beard, a fair pelt moulded to his rubbery little face. His wardrobe includes the uniforms of a Commando, a tank commander, a Red Devil, and a storm-trooper, while he possessed accessories like a rifle rack, a mortar and a belt-feed machine-gun.

He was not dressed in his Commando clothes that Saturday, or in any of his other outfits. He wore a long shirt, borrowed from a teddy bear.

He had been hanged.

It gave me quite a shock to see him. The gallows, made out of Lego, was on two legs with a bar across like a football goal without the net. His hands were tied behind him with knitting wool and the noose was also made out of wool which had been strengthened by being plaited. Rachel and Tommy stood crying, but they didn't touch him. They let him hang, his plastic toes a couple of inches above the cork tiles of the playroom floor. Deirdre looked on serenely.

She didn't object when I cut the Action Man down with nail scissors. Tommy stopped crying, to test his soundbox by pulling a string and listening to him give orders in an American accent, telling his men to go over the top or something similar. Thankfully Anne came back soon after to sort things out. After lunch the rain was still coming down, so they chose to look at television. But that also ended in a row.

'What was it this time?'

Anne said, 'They wouldn't agree on what to watch. Deirdre is becoming impossible. She wouldn't look at the film on RTE and she and Rachel were struggling with the knobs—they almost had the set over. There's only racing or wrestling on the English channels.'

'What was it about? Something horrific? She seems in such a funny state.'

'It was only an old pirate film. Stewart Granger. Deirdre's seen far more grisly things in her time. Remember when we all went to *Jaws*?'

The children continued to bicker so that several times Rachel came to Anne and tried to win her sympathy with a whining tale. Then the television improved, and they sat down silently watching it. I gave Jack a ring, but there was no reply; we concluded that he must have gone down to Naas to fetch his mother-in-law. Anne rang round her friends to find out what their opinion was about giving Deirdre a spot of Valium. I don't know what the verdict was, but the night passed more or less undisturbed. Although the child called out several times, she didn't wake the others, and was deeply asleep the couple of times I went across to her.

When I took her home on Sunday morning Breda's mother was there to greet us. In the kitchen there was a smell of roasting meat, and three of the younger children were seated on the window-seat in front of a table littered with crisp bags, blue tack, Playdough, paper, and felt pens. After giving her grandmother a kiss Deirdre went straight upstairs to the chilly bedrooms above. I accepted a cup of coffee and made stilted conversation with the old lady while I drank. When I finished I said, 'I'd like a word with Jack sometime.'

'He's out front,' she said.

'Oh?'

She let me go and seek him out myself while she attended to the cooking. He was slumped in an armchair in the sitting-room, a couple of unopened Sunday papers beside him. He held a drink and stared out through the double-glazed windows at the rain. He half-turned when he heard the door opening.

'Is that you, Brian? Help yourself.'

'I've had coffee with Mrs Gorman. I brought Deirdre back.'

'She all right?'

I hesitated. 'A bit off colour, we thought.'

'In what way?' His voice was sharp.

'She seemed to be having quite a few nightmares.'

'Anything else?'

120

'Nothing really. Just one or two little things that seemed to indicate she isn't quite herself.'

He wanted to know exactly. He was insistent, so I told him.

'I thought if she got away from the family she might be better . . .'

'What's the matter with her?'

'Do you really want to know?' He immediately began to tell me at length the things he hadn't discussed with the family doctor, the psychiatrist, or the priest. (But later on I ran into a couple of people who had heard the same story from him.) After he had talked for a bit I accepted a drink, and by the end of the morning we had killed the bottle.

He said that the holiday had gone very well—for most of the time. No problems going down, apart from the odd child getting carsick. They went right to the west end of the Dingle peninsula where a farmer near Dunquin rented them a site in a small stonewalled field. There was a view of the sea across the Blaskets towards the pointed peaks of the Skelligs eight or nine miles to the south. The same view they kept showing in *Ryan's Daughter*. The Sprite was a great success—the interior very clean, made more so by Breda. Deirdre and the babies slept in it with their parents, while the two boys had a tent. The weather was perfect and they worked out a routine. Every morning Jack would take all the children down the lane to Krugers to shop while Breda made up the bunks, cleaned the sinkful of Tupperware, and put the washing to soak. After that most days they went to some beach for a picnic. Jack fitted in a good bit of golf. The boys played football while Deirdre spent a lot of time on a school project—collecting shells, or wild flowers which she put in jam-jars or pressed in books.

The sun never stopped shining. A couple of days before they left, the wind died altogether and it became too hot, even in the early morning. The air was stagnant, the sea looked like glue, the Blaskets were turned into sea monster's humps. As they sat round the greasy breakfast plates, the curtains were drawn to keep out the sun.

The boys were shouting for football, while Deirdre wrote neat labels. Breda had a naggy look similar to Deirdre's air of concentration. She was needling Jack about his golf and the round of drinks afterwards that kept him away from his beloved family which would soon be going back to school. Once term began they would see less of their Daddy. He gave in without too much reluctance, because of the heat. He'd made no firm commitment to play. So they got off quite early that day on their picnic.

They left Dunquin, driving past the little mound that is known as Uaig Ri na Spainne—the Grave of the King of Spain—under Mount Eagle and the black claw of Dunmore Head of Coumeenole Bay. About a half-dozen other holiday families were there already. They joined them, taking down the baskets, rugs, and newspapers. Jack put up canvas chairs for himself and Breda and erected the canvas windbreak, more to create a patch of shade than anything. The little white beach, facing south-west, shimmered against the glaring blue of the sunlit water.

Jack and the children swam while Breda cut the bread and divided up the ham and tomatoes and hardboiled eggs, and poured orange squash into plastic mugs. After they had eaten, the parents had their flask of coffee while the children received their daily handout of sweets. Then the elder ones drifted off.

'No more swimming for now,' Jack called as they made their way down to the limp wave line. Breda, wearing dark glasses, read the paper. The babies, in sun hats, pottered near her. Jack slapped lotion on himself.

When he first heard Deirdre's cries he knew it was her straightaway. Sitting up in the glare he looked over the windbreak; he could only pick out two members of his family from the figures strewn along the beach. The boys were standing beside their football which was only visible against the sand because of its hexagonal black markings.

He thought she must be drowning. 'My God, where is she?' He looked seawards; in the distance he could see the fuzzy shape of the Great Blasket, and between it and him the oily current flowing over the Stromboli rocks in a way that seemed to set them moving. He searched the shoreline. The cries were difficult to pinpoint, but people were looking round.

'There!' Breda shrieked. He felt nothing but relief when he located her at last. In fact she was well away from the water, up above the tidemark, a plump little figure standing with her hands over her eyes making this terrible racket. He ran over, Breda gathering up babies and following more slowly. When he got to where she was, her mouth was still wide open in a gape and her eyes were still covered with her hands.

'What is it, darling?' Taking her in his arms, he looked for cuts from broken glass. He had to shout to make himself heard. He couldn't see any blood.

'Stop them!'

'Stop what, treasure?'

'Stop the killing.'

He carried her back towards Breda. A couple of people looked up curiously as Deirdre's wails, making a counterpoint to the song on their transistor, passed them. Gradually her sobs subsided into sniffs and gasps. Once, though, she cried out suddenly, 'They're screaming, Daddy.'

Breda could do nothing with her. She'd be quiet for a bit and then start crying again. She was attracting attention so that in the end they collected everything and drove back. Jack gave up the idea of golf and endured the atmosphere in the stifling caravan for the rest of the day. The babies were fractious, the boys quarrelled, and Deirdre sat huddled on a bunk. Breda thought she might have a spot of sunstroke, but her temperature was normal. Between the fits of sobbing she was almost silent, answering her parents in monosyllables without even a 'Mummy' or 'Daddy' tacked on. If they tried to question her the crying was worse. That night was the first in which she kept calling out in her sleep.

Next day Jack took the boys off, leaving Breda to pack. Deirdre insisted on staying behind with the babies. She did her own version of packing by taking her jam-jars of shells and carrying them over to a ruined cabin that stood on the edge of the field. She threw them all in among the nettles. When Jack was collecting his things together he missed the good leather-handled hammer from his tool-box. He found it easily enough not far from the Sprite, lying beside a stone on which there were the crumbling remains of a substance which he identified as coral from a big piece Deirdre had found on a beach a week before. Stuck to some of it was a piece of lead that had once been round, but was now flattened by blows of the hammer.

When they got back to Dublin Deirdre continued to be difficult. Sometimes she seemed to improve, but then it would be the same thing all over again. The night the weather broke with a thunderstorm she screamed so loudly that a neighbour heard and complained. Her teacher telephoned specially to enquire what was wrong. The family doctor recommended a psychiatrist; there was something of reproach in the hectoring questions he asked them.

'I think his hint that it was all our fault finally drove Breda over the edge.' Jack filled up our glasses. 'He couldn't even make anything out of the drawings.'

'What drawings?'

'I'll show you.' He went over the nylon carpet with its bright pattern of pinwheels to the bookshelf on the right of the rough stone fireplace. Searching among the Reader's Digest condensations, Leon Uris's *Trinity* reverently displayed as if it were indeed a holy book, and the Harold Robbins and Arthur Haileys, he pulled out a stack of library books and finally the *AA Book on Ireland*, which had a wad of papers in it.

'When she got home she did nothing for a few days and then she began to draw. The same thing, time and again. Of course drawings are meat and drink to these boys and he was very interested. He said to encourage her—that drawing would provide a form of therapy which would help her work out her trauma. He asked if Deirdre was a particularly imaginative child in my opinion. Would you say Deirdre was imaginative?'

'No.' He had spread out a number of papers on the coffee table. They showed a crude child's version of an old-fashioned sailing ship with four masts, a high poop, gunports, and flags. It looked very battered.

'He was particularly interested in the torn sails and the crack in the hull. He said that distressed children often convey their feelings in drawings. Most kids like to draw trees and houses. If they do a tree . . . the roots represent the id, the trunk the ego, and the top the super ego.'

'What's that supposed to mean?'

'Jung and his people worked it all out. If the tree is emphasized rather than the roots the child is living in a fantasy world. Look at these ships, the way they float over the waves.'

I looked at them carefully. 'She might just have been trying to convey the effects of a storm.'

'You or I might think so. Not that laddo. He said that a child who has had a traumatic experience within its own family will often draw its house with a crack in it. And sometimes it will put in curtained windows—or cover the windows completely—that is another distress signal. And if it draws trees, another very common theme, they will often have boles which are very much emphasized. Often they will have smoke coming out of them. So your man interpreted these black portholes, and the little bit of smoke at the end of the cannon here and there, and the broken mast and torn sails and all the rest as interesting variations on usual run-of-the-mill disturbed drawings. And he kept asking if Breda and I had had any significant disagreements over the holiday which might have affected the child. It wasn't until a couple of days after I saw him that I realized what nonsense he was talking and that what Deirdre was drawing was a lot of pictures of the *Santa Maria de la Rosa*.'

The books he had with him were Garrett Mattingly's *Defeat of the Spanish Armada*, Evelyn Hardy's *Survivors of the Armada*, and Robert Stenuit's *Treasures of the Armada*. He first opened up the AA book and found an article on marine archaeology which had a clear little diagrammatic illustration. 'For a time I thought Deirdre was just copying from here. Look, she has the same details, the flags and pennant of the Vice Flag Ship of the squadron. And all the different shapes of the sails are right—I've checked. You can make them out, even though she has them torn. All except the foresail. And one mast broken. In every picture.'

His eyes looked glazed. 'She got it all right.' Now he was

referring to passages in the library books marked with dog-eared pages. 'On 13 September 1588 two great ships came down the west coast to just off the Blaskets. They were galleons called the *San Juan de Portugal* and the *San Juan Bautista*. These were two that got away. They anchored for a time, and later set off again, and in the end they got back to Spain. But before that could happen there was a hell of a storm.'

He was referring to another book. 'This storm was on the 21st of September. It swept two other Spanish ships into the sound. One of them was the *Santa Maria de la Rosa*. She was a Mediterranean merchantman that had been specially converted for the Armada. She displaced 945 tons and carried 26 guns. She had a complement of 64 sailors and 233 soldiers. Plenty of gentlemen and proud Spanish hidalgos among them.'

I accepted another glass. He was taking his neat. 'At midday on the 21st she came into the sound nearer land on the north-west side. She fired a shot on entering as if seeking help, and another further on. All her sails were in pieces except the foresail. She anchored, but the anchor dragged and she struck the Stromboli rocks. She sank with all hands, just about.'

'How do they know all this?'

'The captain of the *San Juan Bautista* gave a deposition when he got home to Spain.' He paused. 'I'll tell you a thing about Deirdre. If you try and question her directly it's all dreams and nightmares. But if you ask her about the drawings she doesn't mind. She's usually quite pleased to answer. What do you make of this one?'

He pushed over another sketch of a sailing ship drawn with bright felt pens, the same as the others except that in the wavy blue sea was a black figure with its arms raised.

'When I asked her about him she said, "That's Juan." And I said, "One what?" And she said, very angry. "Not one. Juan. Hoo-an. He's not going to be drowned." That's when I went to the library.' He opened up another reference. 'Seemingly there was just one survivor. They captured him, and before they hanged him he gave evidence.' He read out: 'His ship broke against the rocks in the sound of the Bleskies a league and half from land upon the Tuesday at noon, and all in the ship perished saving this examinate, who saved himself upon two or three planks . . .'

'Oh come on, Jack, she's having you on . . . She's read about it somewhere.'

'She can only just read.'

'Well then, she's learnt about it at school.'

'Breda and I have had to have a couple of sessions with Miss Synott. I asked her specifically if the class had learned anything about the Armada. No, nothing.'

'What about television then?'

'It's possible.' He hardly considered it. 'Here's another, just to show you.' The ship with its torn sails and shattered hull was drawn with a curve of shoreline on which some big curly waves were breaking. The sand, violently yellow, was scattered with what seemed to be piles of black sticks or seaweed.

'No, not seaweed. I asked her. Bodies, she said.'

The last picture he showed me was done with a black pen, and the lack of colour gave it an odd authenticity. This time the little figures had been drawn with great care, and some of them were good enough to put you in mind of Derricke's engravings in the *Image of Ireland*. Jack pointed out details as if it were a holiday snapshot.

'Here's poor old Giovanni or Juan on his gallows in this corner. And this is a group of local militia. These are the Spaniards they are killing.'

The two groups took up the centre of the page, the people on the right thrusting swords into those on the left. Several of the left-hand people were lying prone, within reach of a couple of men bending over them.

'They're stripping them of jewels and weapons.'

'But who are the ones being killed? I thought you said that Giovanni was the only survivor from the *Santa Maria de la Rosa*?'

'He's the only one mentioned in the history books.'

'Who are these supposed to be then?'

'They're more survivors. Deirdre saw them. They went unrecorded. There were thousands of Spaniards off Armada ships being slaughtered all round the west coast, right? When it came to writing down what happened plenty of incidents like this must have been missed out. Giovanni gave evidence that a party went ashore from the *Santa Maria* to try and find water. There's no definite mention of their return. And the captain of the *San Juan Bautista* testified that two days before the storm Admiral Recalde, who was on board his ship, put fifty men ashore in an attempt to get supplies, but they were turned back by some soldiers. He wrote: "100 arquebusiers were marching, bearing a white standard with a red cross. It was concluded that they were English." '

'It seems unlikely they would have waited around for two days.'

'Not at all. We happen to know that there was a detachment of English soldiers at the west end of the Dingle peninsula. It was commanded by a man called James Trent, one of the Sovereign of Dingle's officers. His job was to watch over the Spanish ships anchored off Great Blasket Island. He actually wrote a letter in which he said, "We have two hundred men watching upon the shore every day. We stand in no fear of them"—he meant the Spanish—"for they are so much afraid for themselves." It's clear that Captain Trent's men did a little killing that never made the lists. Look.' Jack showed me another of Deirdre's pictures—a small group of soldiers, three of whom held old-fashioned guns with trumpet-like barrels. 'Arquebuses.' Another carried a standard with a red cross. It was the only bit of colour in the whole picture.

'I must go,' I said. 'Lunch will be waiting.'

12

MAURICE LEITCH

Green Roads

The old man was sitting on the bus seat buried in the bank outside his cottage when the army landrover went past in the late afternoon. It churned up the steep slope in the direction of the bog where no wheeled traffic had ever been known to go before and, as it topped the incline, the old man saw a soldier with a black face staring out at him over the tail-board. The colour was natural, not camouflage, he could tell, even though it was his very first negro. This darkie soldier held a rifle and looked straight through him as if he didn't exist. The old man sat pondering in the dying sunlight. Something, he didn't know what, held him back from going inside to tell his daughter what he had seen, yet seldom did anything like this ever happen to him. One day followed another in the same dreamlike fashion, day after day after day spent here on this old summer-seat. He stroked its warm, worn upholstery. His daughter kept saying his memory was going but it was more a case of not being able to make it do his bidding, for something remembered, but deeply submerged, about men in uniform passing this way once before refused stubbornly to surface. He would just have to wait until the memory, whatever it was, floated up of its own accord. It was just that you could never tell when; perhaps today, perhaps tomorrow, perhaps never.

The old man looked at a distant staining of smoke in the evening sky. Someone had started to burn whins on their land. The others would follow suit now, he told himself; there always had to be one to start the first fire somewhere or other, for the rest to follow.

The driver of the landrover was a corporal named Jessop from Devizes in Wiltshire, unmarried, in his early thirties, with the reputation for keeping himself to himself. A self-contained character, some would even say dour, but then that may have been because of his background. Everyone else in the platoon seemed to be from an industrial Northern city and took much pleasure in reminding him of that fact. Even Carlton, despite the colour of his skin, would chance his luck now and again, slyly joining in. Coming from Streatham put him on an equal footing with the others, as far as he was concerned.

At the corporal's side rode the young lieutenant who had the map spread on his knees. The landrover bucked and bounced and Carlton in the rear swore fluently but the corporal stared straight ahead. A perverse pleasure was making him aim for every bump and pothole in their path for he knew that they were lost and this track they were on led nowhere. The young lieutenant, however, would not admit to the fact. It was part of his class 'thing': something the other two recognized.

On either side stretched desolate moorland the colour of the vehicle they travelled in, without break or respite for the eye. They passed sheep with splashes of dye on their fleece but they kept their heads resolutely lowered. Carlton aimed his rifle taking silent pot-shots but even he seemed to feel their chill disregard. Light rain began to fall and the rhythm of the windscreen wipers beat time with their thoughts, or it may have been the other way round, while a mood of gloom settled on the landrover and its three occupants. It was as if it had shrunk or been reduced in some way to the size of an insect crawling along under a vast and darkening sky.

There came a stretch when all heard the sump drag itself over the long, stony ridge that now seemed to bisect the track. Jessop put his foot hard on the brake and sat looking out at the gathering dusk until the lieutenant said, 'Yes, let's stop here. Get our bearings, shall we?' He marched to the front and spread his map on the bonnet and began to pore over the brown and green contours.

Carlton sang softly, 'I was onlee twentee-four hours from

Tulsa,' until Jessop told him to be quiet. Then the lieutenant was waving him over and together they studied the map.

'You can see we're roughly here,' said the lieutenant, his finger on a line of dots hugging the contours.

Jessop noted that there were quite a number of these fine lines curving and snaking across the terrain. 'Sheep paths, sir?'

'Definitely not. No question. Perfectly passable routes each and every one of them. If we stay with this one we're on, as you can see, we'll strike this secondary road here and then it's only a matter of time before we're on course for base. The map is perfectly clear about that.'

'When was it made, sir? The map, I mean.'

The lieutenant looked at him. 'No one has more up-to-date information than we have, corporal, always remember that.'

They climbed back into the landrover and Carlton said, 'How far now?' but no one answered him. They drove on and for a time the track seemed to be improving. The lieutenant handed cigarettes around, even joked a little, and Carlton sang the whole of his song now without any trace of irony.

Then they began to descend, slowly at first but finally in a rush, scattering countless small stones loosened by the rain. These rattled off the metal beneath their feet with a noise like gunfire and the corporal went even faster as though fleeing from an invisible attacker. That was how the young lieutenant saw it. An imaginative side to his nature still lingered even after all his training. But the reality was that Jessop had spotted a steep incline ahead, one in ten at least to his eyes, despite the visibility, and he wanted to tackle it at speed. But, as it turned out, it was to be the dip at the base of both hills that was to prove their undoing. With engine roaring the landrover bounded downhill and raced across the flat stretch of track. At first their route seemed smooth, almost finished in fact, but then the corporal noticed that the wheels were slowing as though some exterior force was at work. He pressed the accelerator but the engine only screamed on a higher, more maddened note. At a point half-way along this valley floor the landrover finally came to a halt, its rear wheels spinning in troughs of mud.

The lieutenant sat stiff and silent while Carlton in the back swore and gave advice. Jessop, who was an experienced driver and proud of his skills, went through every combination of gears before finally switching off the engine.

The lieutenant said, 'Is there a problem, corporal?' Carlton laughed. 'We do have four-wheel drive, don't we?'

'Correct, sir.'

'So, why do we have a problem?'

Jessop sighed and got out. Kneeling down he stared blankly at a wheel, noting with no real interest that it was already buried to the hub and appeared to be sinking. His own boots were, as well, a strange sensation and, straightening up, he walked off a few paces leaving behind well-defined tracks. The ground had a curious consistency, not quite solid. The corporal lifted a large flat rock and pitched it several yards then watched it settle in the hollow it had formed.

Standing there he was barely conscious of the fine rain on his face, or anything else for that matter. The landrover and its occupants and their plight meant nothing to him. He might have been one of those sheep they had passed earlier. He didn't feel angry, as might be expected. Instead, as he listened to the silence he felt inert as stone.

Then the young lieutenant joined him making a great play of kicking the tyres and stooping to peer underneath. The corporal stared at the back of his head, young and vulnerable under his beret, and he felt dizzy for a moment, sweating at the sudden and unexplained violence of his thoughts.

The lieutenant straightened up. 'Have we anything we can put down, an old blanket, tarpaulin, that sort of thing?'

'Not really, sir. We can't get purchase.'

'I can see that for myself, corporal.' Carlton had joined them and both he and the lieutenant were looking expectantly at Jessop now.

The the lieutenant said, 'Get me the machete, private,' and Carlton, suddenly energetic and grinning, brought it to him in its canvas sheath. 'We'll make a start by cutting some of this gorse. If it works in snow I don't see why it shouldn't do the trick in this muck as well.'

He slid out the greased blade—it had never been used—and held it out to neither of them in particular, but Jessop turned away almost fastidiously. Then Carlton seized it and began hacking at the tough stalks.

The lieutenant watched the growing pile. He was remembering with fondness one Boxing night when his MG had got stuck not far from Dorking. While the other three had laughed and continued to drink in the car he had worked like a demon among the drifts foraging and, finally, bedding the wheels with bracken and although it had been a sudden impulse on his part it had done the trick. Much later he had found out, indirectly, that the girls in particular had been most impressed but it was his own private pleasure that meant more to him, despite having ruined a perfectly good dinner-jacket.

With the mood of that snowy night still upon him he began furiously laying armfuls of the stuff around and under all four wheels. Then he stamped and pounded with his boots until the landrover seemed to be resting on a thick, sodden, brown carpet. Carlton stood watching, as did Jessop, but when he tried to signal to the corporal his amusement at the sight of this odd war dance the other turned his face away.

The lieutenant shouted, 'Let's see if *that* will do the trick!' and Jessop went over to the landrover and climbed in. For a moment he sat there as though he had never seen a dashboard or steering wheel in his life before, then, shaking his head violently, he pressed the starter. All his old skills returned to him and with infinite patience he began coaxing the engine to its task.

For a long time he hung in the seat oblivious to everything but the sounds of the motor and the straining of the transmission then, above the roar, he heard someone shouting his name and the lieutenant was at the open door. The corporal looked at him in surprise. His face and front were coated with mud, great gouts of it. Why was he shouting, the corporal asked himself. He was genuinely confused. The lieutenant reached in and switched off the engine, then began wiping his face with his coarse mesh scarf. He spat disgustedly. Carlton came into view, winking at Jessop. 'Your driving, corp, blimey!'

The lieutenant said, 'What a God-awful, bloody country,' then he looked at Jessop who still sat grasping the wheel. 'I really think you've done enough for one day, corporal, don't you?' and his voice had taken on the leisurely drawl of his class, something the two men had never heard before.

'Looks as if we're bogged down then, sir,' said Carlton cheerfully. 'What we need is a tow.'

The lieutenant stared about him. 'Smoke over there.' He sniffed as if he could smell it. 'Now, if they have a tractor . . .'

Jessop had got out by now and, speaking quietly as if to the ground, said, 'No tractors. Not out here, not these people.'

The other two exchanged glances. Carlton was grinning again but the lieutenant's face had set hard as stone. 'Yes, you *would* know all about that, wouldn't you, Jessop?'

Then he reached under the passenger seat, pulling out the handset of the radio. They listened to him talking to base, explaining their plight and position on the map, and at first his voice was patient and unhurried just as if he was speaking to one of them. But then there were angry blizzards of static from the other end and they could hear him protesting.

At one point he said, 'Some joker must have turned the signposts around, sir,' and it registered with Jessop even in his dulled state that he had been right about the lieutenant all along. But there was no satisfaction in the knowledge. He was standing a little way off by himself with his head raised as if he was picking up signals of his own from the air.

They were in a glen of sorts, ringed on all sides by moorland, the rim blue-black and clearly defined against the sky. The low murmur of running water could be heard nearby. Jessop felt something he could not put into words. It was as if he had stood like this in such a place once before in a dream. For a dizzy moment he seemed to be looking down on to the scene from a great height, the landrover the size of a matchbox toy, himself a figure tiny in scale a little way off. He felt, he felt—it seemed to him he was on the point of getting to the secret core of it when the moment passed and the lieutenant shouted for him to return to the land-rover.

He was sitting in the front with a look on his face that said he would be doing everything strictly by the book from now on. 'No tow truck until o-nine-hundred hours, I'm afraid.'

The grin left Carlton's face. *'Tomorrow!'*

The lieutenant ignored him. 'So it looks like a night on the bare mountain for us all, chaps.' A wintry little smile at his private joke came and went.

'Jesus Christ, sir!' Carlton cried out. 'Not out *here!*' His grip had tightened on his weapon while his eyes went darting about him.

'Oh, relax, private, you're not in bandit country now. Certainly not around here. Believe me, I do know.' And he did, for it was something he took pride in, the young lieutenant, his 'demography', as he liked to call it back in the mess.

'I don't care a toss what side they're on, you can 'ave 'em! Bleedin' sheep-shaggers, the lot of them!'

The lieutenant laughed, looking at Jessop as he did so, but the corporal had returned once more to his own private world.

'Come,' said the lieutenant, jumping out of the landrover, 'we must build a shelter before it gets too dark.'

Carlton grounded his rifle in disbelief. 'Shelter! Sir?'

The lieutenant held out the machete, but this time it was clear that it was intended for Jessop. For a moment the corporal weighed it in his hand, looking at it strangely, then he began clearing a patch a little way off where the ground was firm. The corporal worked slightly bent at one knee, the blade cutting low and close, and there was such economy and ease about the operation that the other two watched in silence. Heaps of the tawny gorse began to rise about the sides of a perfectly formed rectangle. The revealed sward was pale and cropped and the lieutenant stared at its perfection. An anger was growing in him for what he and the private were witnessing was nothing more, it seemed to him, than yet another ploy intended to make him look foolish.

'All right,' he managed to call out at last. 'All right, you've made your point!' but Jessop continued to work on.

The lieutenant's face became redder. Rising, he strode across to the toiler, laying a hand on his shoulder. Instantly he felt the heat of the man's body through the khaki wool and, in the same moment, Jessop jerked as though stung. Then he raised a face with such savagery in it that the lieutenant fell back. They both looked down at the blade in the corporal's hand, then the moment passed.

The lieutenant called out, 'We'll bed down here,' striking a heel deep in the turf. Then he made off in the direction of the stream, tracking it by sound, for he felt certain there would be saplings growing there, and he was right, too. But before doing a thing he carefully wiped the haft of the machete and his own hands to remove all traces of the corporal's sweat.

Carlton said, 'Answer me one question, just one question,' when the lieutenant disappeared from sight. 'Why can't we just kip in the 'rover? I mean, did we join the boy scouts, or what?' He offered Jessop a smoke from his tin but the corporal declined.

'No?' said the other, then he leaned close. 'Here, what you on, man? You're on something, ain't you, sly old sod.'

The corporal got up from the bumper and moved back to the space he had just cleared. He stood there at its heart while Carlton continued to eye him slyly.

'Give us a taste, man,' came that soft voice. ''Cause I know you're on something, that's for sure.'

Jessop turned his head away as if to hide the evidence, though the truth was that he had taken nothing, never had for that matter. Something deep-seated had always made him shy clear of such things, even now when the right pill could see him through this. For two weeks he hadn't slept. He wondered how long he would be able to keep going. A numbness and a trembling had begun in one of his legs and he knew his reactions were slowing, but he didn't want any help from anything or anyone. The word punishment entered his head for some reason. He supposed this must be his way of punishing himself, his body, for that night in the pub car-park near Swindon. He closed his eyes, breathing in deeply, willing himself to remember. The images began to burn.

It had been the last night of his leave and it had been a pub picked at random, not that he was a great one for pubs, never had been, but before going back for another tour of duty something made him walk into this place in the heart of the country. He had imagined what it might be like inside, horse-brasses, oak settles, a real fire of logs even, and it was as he'd pictured it, something to remember over there, take the edge off things when it all started getting you down. He ordered a pint and sat in a corner out of the way, a habit, when he heard this man at the bar. There were other people in the place as well, regulars, but the man's accent, although it was soft, seemed to go through him like a knife. He began to tremble, he didn't know why, sitting there with his tankard in front of him, and as the time passed and the stranger with the brogue began to talk more and more loudly he found he couldn't rise to go up for a refill. He just listened and shook with lowered eyes. Nothing like this had ever happened to him before, such a terrible hatred for a complete stranger. There seemed no answer to it. The man was neither a bully nor loudmouth; he seemed genuinely liked in the place. It was obvious, too, that he was country-bred, like everyone else there, himself included, nothing could disguise it. At one point he did cry out passionately, 'Don't call me *Pat*. I'm not a *Pat*. I'm as British as the rest of you. Nobody knows our history. *Our* history. Or cares,' and they all laughed at him. Then he laughed, too, and ordered a round for the house and Jessop, in his corner, knew it was time to go for he felt he mustn't allow his hate to be diluted, so he quickly rose and walked out.

In the car-park in the dark he waited for almost an hour, it seemed, before the man came out to relieve himself. He was singing, something sad like all their songs, and even when Jessop felled him he still continued to sing a little. Then the kicking began in earnest, for the corporal had been trained to inflict the utmost damage as speedily and as effectively as possible and he had been taught well, yet the man curled up on the ground barely uttered a sound, a protest or cry, even, while it was happening to him. Almost as if he felt he deserved it in some strange way.

That was a fortnight ago and he had walked off into the night not knowing or caring if the heap on the ground was alive or dead. The following day he was back on patrol, over here, on the stranger's own terrain.

The corporal looked down now at the carefully mown patch of turf at his feet. Punishment. The word came into his head again. How long must he have to wait? Not long now, he told himself, almost soothingly, not long now, for it seemed to him, standing here in this place, that he had already prepared the ground for it.

Returning with his booty the young lieutenant saw the corporal standing there as though defending his newly acquired territory. The sight displeased him for some reason and he shouted out for him to come and give a hand, dropping his burden where it lay. At the stream, he had carefully trimmed, then pointed the stakes and the look of them lying together now so healthy and still full of sap filled him with pride. Already he could smell the never to be forgotten tang of his old tree-hut in the garden at Weybridge.

He watched while Carlton and the corporal constructed a rough shelter using the materials at hand and when it met finally with his approval they all stood back to look at it. Darkness had crept up and with it a chill mist. Carlton shivered dramatically. 'How's about a nice little fire, then, sir?'

'No fire. No lights.' The lieutenant's face seemed to have lost its youthful outline in the little light remaining.

'But you said it was all right, sir. Out here, sir. No bandits, remember, sir?'

'I know I did. Another thing, no smoking, either. I'll take the first watch.'

He waited until they crawled inside the makeshift bothy before going over to lean against the side of the grounded landrover. First watch, he knew, was the soft one to draw but he didn't care, that was his prerogative. He was piqued, as well, if the truth were known because, too late, he'd realized that he would have to share his hut, when what he really wanted all along was to have it all to himself the way he remembered it from those long magical school holidays.

Carlton and the corporal lay in the close, itchy darkness, side by side, not talking, because they both knew the lieutenant was only a matter of yards away. A low moaning sound was the nearest Carlton could get to his greatest desire which was to complain loudly and at length. He tossed and turned on their bed of bracken while the corporal lay unmoving, staring up at a gap in the low roof. Presently a star could be seen framed there. It looked like an eye to the corporal but the thought didn't disturb him. Ever since they had arrived in this place he had felt he was being watched. All he could do now was wait, he told himself, for whatever was out there to catch up with him. It was only a matter of time.

At midnight by his watch the lieutenant put his head into the darkness of the shelter. Carlton was snoring steadily, the corporal lay alongside, silent as a log, and the lieutenant smiled to himself, for the past four hours on his own had, strangely enough, smoothed away all his earlier vexation. These were his men, he thought fondly to himself, see how they depended on him. The way they slept out here in this place so trustingly was the measure of that. He decided he was a lucky man after all, that he really had found his true vocation. He put out a searching hand to grasp Carlton's ankle, it really had to be done, when he felt another hand take his before it could close on the sleeper's foot. A voice from the darkness said quietly, 'I'll take the next watch, sir,' and the corporal's body slid swiftly past and out into the night air before he had time to think or make any sort of reply.

A full moon had come out by this time and Jessop felt dwarfed by the glare. He hunkered down; his shadow contracted even more. Far off somewhere the cry of an animal in pain quickly came and went and he was left to his watch.

As he crouched there, everything about him seemed to imprint itself upon his brain with terrible clarity as if he could read the landscape like no one else before or since. Grasping a tussock of grass to anchor himself he saw how the encircling rim of hills ran with barely a dip in its outline even where the track entered and left it, and the track itself had a similar perfection of line. It brought to mind old Roman routes from his own part of the country yet he had read that no Roman had ever set foot here. Before, it had lain there barely visible to the eye but now, by this trick of the light, the path had come back into its own. He thought of all those other old forgotten tracks lying hidden on the lieutenant's map and only returning to life like this while people slept.

The lethargy had left him now; his brain felt clear and responsive. He looked at the landrover, then at the shelter where the others were sleeping, oblivious. The landrover looked as though it had sunk even further, was still sinking, in fact. As for the shelter, it seemed reclaimed already; nothing but a handful of sticks and dying grasses. The corporal knew with total certainty now that he would never leave this place. It was an irony, even though it barely registered, for it to happen to him out here, he thought, in such a setting, and not in some alleyway in the city he had left that morning, the way he'd always expected it to be. And so he waited almost calmly, for he knew he could take the last watch as well if it was to take that long.

But then something strange and most unusual happened. The corporal fell asleep out there in the open and when he awoke, stiff and damp, the moon had gone and in its place a ribbon of light was beginning to brighten the sky to the east. He rubbed his eyes and tried to get up from where he had fallen. Instinct made him reach out in a panic for his weapon but it was there by his side, wet to the touch. Then he looked up and, where the distant rim of the high moor was turning to pink, he saw a number of objects breaking its outline. They looked like fencing posts at first, but then he saw that they weren't spaced evenly and that they varied in height and bulk as well. He shielded his gaze with his hand, squinting into the growing light, and then at last he saw what they were. At least thirty motionless figures stood there looking down at him and even at that distance he could feel the terrible intensity of their gaze. There was great patience there as well, it seemed to him, as if, while he slept, they had waited without movement or complaint. He began to notice other things as well. Most of them held implements in their hands, a few scythes, but mainly pitchforks and long poles tipped with metal. Their clothes looked outlandish as well, old and worn out from the effect of weather and long drudgery in the open.

Jessop, the corporal from Wiltshire, stood there as though on trial but already knowing the verdict. He felt calm and curiously rested. The watchers on the horizon had made no move but by now he knew they never would. There was a great silence all around. It was time. The corporal knelt down and, taking off his beret, laid it on the ground by his side. He took up his rifle. Its metal was cold and damp to the touch from where it had lain on the grass and, as he brought the barrel up under his chin, the last thing to reach his senses was the pungent odour of gun-oil.

Propped up in bed—it was the only way he could sleep now he found—the old man came sharply out of a fitful dream. He listened for the sound that had woken him to come a second time but it refused. A sharp crack like the snap of a dry twig but distant, very distant, that was all the impression he was left with. The window was brightening now: he watched the room take form. At this hour he had only his thoughts to occupy him, his daughter wouldn't stir until her alarm went off in the middle of the morning, so he allowed memories, fragments of the past, free play.

On the wall facing him was a posed photograph of his own father holding a Union Jack and a curved ornamental sword. He could barely remember him yet, strangely, everything about his grandfather would always fall into sharp focus. He had been thinking about him only last night in the kitchen and about the way he had of slowly lifting live coals out of the fire between finger and thumb to light his pipe, when it had come to him about the soldiers going up the bog road. It was a story from the old, almost forgotten days when every house had a pike buried in the thatch in readiness for the call. Then, after the big battle and the rout, a troop of Fencibles, that was the name his grandfather had called them, were supposed to have ridden past this way in pursuit of some rebels, another unusual name for people from these parts. But the English troopers had got caught in the bog, men and horses sinking, so the story went, deep in the moss, and after a time the men in brown coats, as they were known, came down from the high ground and piked all of them to death. No trace had ever been found, not a bone or a belt buckle. All that remained was an old story, for the bog never gave up any of its secrets.

The old man thought of the road; he hadn't been that way for twenty years. It used to be a beautiful, wild place even then. In time no one would even remember that a track had once run that way. It would all go back to its original state; soon he, himself, would be joining it. The old man wept a little, for no one likes to contemplate that sort of thing without some sadness.

BIOGRAPHICAL NOTES

1

CECIL FRANCES ALEXANDER (1818–95). Born in Dublin and brought up in Co. Tyrone. Wife of the Bishop of Derry (later Archbishop of Armagh), and a noted hymn-writer whose works include 'All Things Bright and Beautiful' and 'There is a Green Hill Far Away'. Author of many religious verses—*Hymns for Little Children* was published in 1848—and one oddity, the retelling in an Ulster-Scots dialect of a Donegal ghost story, 'The Legend of Stumpie's Brae', which is her most robust composition.

2

JOSEPH SHERIDAN LE FANU (1814–73). Born in Dublin. Barrister, novelist, and short-story writer whose best-known work, *Uncle Silas*, was published in 1864. His supernatural stories, beginning with 'The Ghost and the Bone-Setter' in 1838, quickly gained him a reputation as the leading Irish practitioner in this field.

3

CHARLOTTE RIDDELL (1832–1906). Born in Carrickfergus, Co. Antrim. Moved to London in 1856. A popular Victorian novelist and magazine editor, who contributed many tales of the uncanny to Christmas annuals and the like. Author of some classic ghost stories including 'The Old House at Vauxhall Walk', as well as one or two which draw on her Irish background.

4

ROSA MULHOLLAND (Lady Gilbert) (1841–1921). Daughter of Joseph Stevenson Mulholland. Born into an upper-middle-class Catholic family in Belfast. Wrote many novels of Irish peasant life, with titles like *The Wild Birds of Killeevy*. Her tales of the supernatural, many of which originally appeared in Dickens's magazine *All the Year Round*, were collected in 1888 in *The Haunted Organist of Hurly Burly*.

5

GEORGE MOORE (1852–1933). Born at Moore Hall, Co. Mayo. Novelist, autobiographer, and short-story writer, and a leading figure in the Irish Literary Revival. His short-story collection of 1903, *The Untilled Field*—which includes 'A Play-House in the Waste'—is held, along with Joyce's *Dubliners*, to have brought a new realism and starkness to the Irish story. *Hail and Farewell* (1911–14) is the title of his three-volume autobiography-cum-history of the Revival.

6

FORREST REID (1875–1947). Born in Belfast. Critic and novelist, whose primary theme was boyhood and adolescence; best known for his 'Tom Barber' trilogy (1931–44). An unacknowledged homosexual who lived as a near-recluse in Belfast. Wrote a couple of autobiographies, *Apostate* (1926) and *Private Road* (1940), and the collection of short stories—*The Garden by the Sea* (1918)—from which 'Courage' is taken.

7

DOROTHY MACARDLE (1889–1958). Born in Dundalk. Historian, novelist, and short-story writer, and author of the official history of the War of Independence, *The Irish Republic* (1937). Imprisoned for republican activities in 1922, she drew on this experience for the stories collected in *Earth-Bound*, published in the same year.

8

ELIZABETH BOWEN (1899–1973). Born in Dublin. Anglo-Irish novelist, critic, essayist, and woman of letters, and one of the most distinguished short-story writers of the century. Her output includes a number of ghost stories, of which 'The Happy Autumn Fields' (in the wartime collection *The Demon Lover*, 1945) is one of the most riveting and evocative.

9

J. F. BYRNE (1880–1955). Born in Dublin. Moved to New York in 1911, where he became a reporter and daily columnist with the *New York Times* and other papers. A friend of James Joyce at Dublin University, and the original of 'Cranly' in *A Portrait of the Artist as a Young Man*. Wrote an autobiography, *Silent Years* (1953)—subtitled 'with Memoirs of James Joyce and our Ireland'—from which ' "Ghosts" in House on Cork Hill' is taken.

10

SIR SHANE LESLIE (1885–1971). Born Co. Monaghan. A prolific author, whose works include biographical studies, poetry, and fiction.

11

PETER SOMERVILLE-LARGE (1928–   ). Author, travel writer, and social historian. Born in Dublin and educated at Trinity College. After working abroad for a time, he returned to Ireland in the 1960s and now lives in County Kilkenny. He is the author of *The Irish Country House: A Social History* (1995) and *Dublin: The Fair City* (1996).

12

MAURICE LEITCH (1933–   ). Born in Co. Antrim. Novelist and short-story writer. Has worked as a teacher and a BBC producer in Belfast and London. First novel, *The Liberty Lad*, published in 1965.

SOURCE ACKNOWLEDGEMENTS

George Moore, 'A Play-house in the Waste' from *The Untilled Field* (1903). Reproduced by permission of Colin Smythe Limited on behalf of the heirs of the Literary Estate of George Moore.

Forrest Reid, 'Courage' from *A Garden By The Sea* (1918). Reproduced by kind permission of John Johnson Ltd., London, on behalf of the executors of the Estate of Forrest Reid.

Elizabeth Bowen, 'The Happy Autumn Fields' from *The Demon Lover and Other Stories*, Jonathan Cape (1945). Also from *Collected Stories* by Elizabeth Bowen copyright © 1981 by Curtis Brown Ltd., Literary Executors of the Estate of Elizabeth Bowen. Reprinted by permission of Alfred A. Knopf Inc.

J. F. Byrne, '"Ghosts" in House on Cork Hill' from *Silent Years* (1953); copyright renewed © 1981 by J. F. Byrne. Reprinted by permission of Farrar, Straus & Giroux Inc.

Maurice Leitch, 'Green Roads' from *The Hands of Cheryl Boyd and Other Stories* (1987). Copyright © Maurice Leitch 1989. Reproduced by permission of the author and Rogers, Coleridge & White Ltd.

OXFORD

MORE OXFORD PAPERBACKS

This book is just one of nearly 1000 Oxford Paperbacks currently in print. If you would like details of other Oxford Paperbacks, including titles in the World's Classics, Oxford Reference, Oxford Books, OPUS, Past Masters, Oxford Authors, and Oxford Shakespeare series, please write to:

UK and Europe: Oxford Paperbacks Publicity Manager, Arts and Reference Publicity Department, Oxford University Press, Walton Street, Oxford OX2 6DP.

Customers in UK and Europe will find Oxford Paperbacks available in all good bookshops. But in case of difficulty please send orders to the Cash-with-Order Department, Oxford University Press Distribution Services, Saxon Way West, Corby, Northants NN18 9ES. Tel: 01536 741519; Fax: 01536 746337. Please send a cheque for the total cost of the books, plus £1.75 postage and packing for orders under £20; £2.75 for orders over £20. Customers outside the UK should add 10% of the cost of the books for postage and packing.

USA: Oxford Paperbacks Marketing Manager, Oxford University Press, Inc., 200 Madison Avenue, New York, N.Y. 10016.

Canada: Trade Department, Oxford University Press, 70 Wynford Drive, Don Mills, Ontario M3C 1J9.

Australia: Trade Marketing Manager, Oxford University Press, G.P.O. Box 2784Y, Melbourne 3001, Victoria.

South Africa: Oxford University Press, P.O. Box 1141, Cape Town 8000.

OXFORD PAPERBACK REFERENCE

From *Art and Artists* to *Zoology*, the Oxford Paperback Reference series offers the very best subject reference books at the most affordable prices.

Authoritative, accessible, and up to date, the series features dictionaries in key student areas, as well as a range of fascinating books for a general readership. Included are such well-established titles as Fowler's *Modern English Usage*, Margaret Drabble's *Concise Companion to English Literature*, and the bestselling science and medical dictionaries.

The series has now been relaunched in handsome new covers. Highlights include new editions of some of the most popular titles, as well as brand new paperback reference books on *Politics*, *Philosophy*, and *Twentieth-Century Poetry*.

With new titles being constantly added, and existing titles regularly updated, Oxford Paperback Reference is unrivalled in its breadth of coverage and expansive publishing programme. New dictionaries of *Film*, *Economics*, *Linguistics*, *Architecture*, *Archaeology*, *Astronomy*, and *The Bible* are just a few of those coming in the future.

Oxford
Paperback
Reference

THE CONCISE OXFORD DICTIONARY
OF MATHEMATICS

New Edition

Edited by Christopher Clapham

Authoritative and reliable, this is the ideal reference guide for students of mathematics at school or in the first year at university. Nearly 1,000 entries have been added for this new edition and the dictionary provides clear definitions, with helpful examples, of a wide range of mathematical terms and concepts.

* **Covers both pure and applied mathematics as well as statistics.**

* **Entries on the great mathematicians**

* **Coverage of mathematics of more general interest, including fractals, game theory, and chaos**

'the depth of information provided is admirable'
New Scientist

'the style encourages browsing and a desire to find out more about the topics discussed'
Mathematica

POPULAR SCIENCE FROM OXFORD PAPERBACKS

THE SELFISH GENE

Second Edition

Richard Dawkins

Our genes made us. We animals exist for their preservation and are nothing more than their throwaway survival machines. The world of the selfish gene is one of savage competition, ruthless exploitation, and deceit. But what of the acts of apparent altruism found in nature—the bees who commit suicide when they sting to protect the hive, or the birds who risk their lives to warn the flock of an approaching hawk? Do they contravene the fundamental law of gene selfishness? By no means: Dawkins shows that the selfish gene is also the subtle gene. And he holds out the hope that our species—alone on earth—has the power to rebel against the designs of the selfish gene. This book is a call to arms. It is both manual and manifesto, and it grips like a thriller.

The Selfish Gene, Richard Dawkins's brilliant first book and still his most famous, is an international bestseller in thirteen languages. For this greatly expanded edition, endnotes have been added, giving fascinating reflections on the original text, and there are two major new chapters.

'learned, witty, and very well written . . . exhilaratingly good.' Sir Peter Medawar, *Spectator*

'Who should read this book? Everyone interested in the universe and their place in it.' Jeffrey R. Baylis, *Animal Behaviour*

'the sort of popular science writing that makes the reader feel like a genius' *New York Times*

OXFORD LIVES

'SUBTLE IS THE LORD'

The Science and the Life of Albert Einstein

Abraham Pais

Abraham Pais, an award-winning physicist who knew Einstein personally during the last nine years of his life, presents a guide to the life and the thought of the most famous scientist of our century. Using previously unpublished papers and personal recollections from their years of acquaintance, the narrative illuminates the man through his work with both liveliness and precision, making this *the* authoritative scientific biography of Einstein.

'The definitive life of Einstein.' Brian Pippard, *Times Literary Supplement*

'By far the most important study of both the man and the scientist.' Paul Davies, *New Scientist*

'An outstanding biography of Albert Einstein that one finds oneself reading with sheer pleasure.' *Physics Today*